Ellery Queen's
COPS AND CAPERS

Ellery Queen's

COPS
AND
CAPERS

Edited by Ellery Queen

DAVIS PUBLICATIONS, INC.
229 Park Avenue South
New York, N.Y. 10003

COPYRIGHT NOTICES AND ACKNOWLEDGMENTS

Grateful acknowledgment is hereby made for permission to reprint
the following:

The Dazzle Dan Murder Case by Rex Stout; copyright 1952 by Rex
Stout; reprinted by permission of the author.

The Light Next Door by Charlotte Armstrong; © 1968 by Charlotte Armstrong; reprinted by permission of Brandt & Brandt.

The Empty Birdhouse by Patricia Highsmith; © 1968 by Patricia
Highsmith; reprinted by permission of McIntosh & Otis, Inc.

'Twixt the Cup and the Lip by Julian Symons; © Julian Symons
1963; reprinted by permission of Curtis Brown, Ltd.

The Insomniacs Club by John Lutz; © 1968 by John Lutz; reprinted by permission of Scott Meredith Literary Agency, Inc.

Not Easy To Kill by Philip Wylie; copyright 1935 by Crowell Pub-
lishing Company, copyright renewed 1963 by Philip Wylie; reprinted by permission of Harold Ober Associates, Inc.

CONTENTS

by REX STOUT

THE DAZZLE DAN
MURDER CASE

*Like so many of Nero Wolfe's cases, this one looked simple
and ordinary; but like so many of Nero Wolfe's cases, it proved anything but—before you could say Archie Goodwin, the
case became complicated and extraordinary. And like all of
Nero Wolfe's cases, it parades a fascinating cast of characters: Harry Koven, the curiously indecisive creator of Dazzle
Dan, famous comic-strip hero; his much younger wife; a
strange little man called Squirt; Koven's Girl Friday, his
agent and business manager; the two artists who actually
drew Dazzle Dan; and last but definitely not least, a tropical
monkey called Rookaloo.*

*Near the end of this short novel, complete in this anthol-
ogy, and just before the denouement, Archie thinks that
Nero Wolfe's efforts are "far from one of his best
performances"—in a case "where nothing less than his best
would do." Well, Archie has eaten his words before: Nero
Wolfe triumphs again! . . .*

I was doing two things at once. With my hands I was getting my armpit holster and the Marley .32 from a
drawer of my desk, and with my tongue I was giving Nero
Wolfe a lecture on economics.

"The most you can hope to soak him," I stated, "is five
hundred bucks. Deduct a C for overhead and another C for
expenses incurred, that leaves three hundred. Eighty-five
per cent for income tax will leave you with forty-five bucks
clear for the wear and tear on your brain and my legs, not
to mention the risk. That wouldn't buy—"

"Risk of what?" He muttered that only to be courteous, to
show that he had heard what I said, though actually he
wasn't listening. Seated behind his desk, he was scowling,
not at me but at the crossword puzzle in the London *Times*.

"Complications," I said darkly. "You heard him explain it. Playing games with a gun is sappy." I was contorted, buckling the strap of the holster. That done, I picked up my coat. "Since you're listed in the red book as a detective, and since I draw pay, such as it is, as your licensed assistant, I'm all for detecting for people on request. But this bozo wants to do it himself, using our firearm as a prop. We might just as well send it up to him by messenger."

"Pfui," Wolfe muttered. "It is a thoroughly conventional proceeding. You are merely out of humor because you don't like Dazzle Dan. If it were Pleistocene Polly you would be zealous."

"Nuts. I look at the comics occasionally just to be cultured. It wouldn't hurt any if you did."

I went to the hall for my things, let myself out, descended the stoop, and headed toward Tenth Avenue for a taxi. A cold gusty wind came at my back from across the Hudson, and I made it brisk, swinging my arms, to get my blood going.

It was true that I did not care for Dazzle Dan, the hero of the comic strip that was syndicated to two thousand newspapers—or was it two million?—throughout the land. Also I did not care for his creator, Harry Koven, who had called at the office Saturday evening, forty hours ago. He had kept chewing his upper lip with jagged yellow teeth, and it had seemed to me that he might at least have chewed the lower lip instead of the upper, which doesn't show teeth. Moreover, I had not cared for his job as he outlined it. Not that I was getting snooty about the renown of Nero Wolfe—a guy who has had a gun lifted has got as much right to buy good detective work as a rich duchess accused of murder—but the way this Harry Koven had programmed it he was going to do the detecting himself, so the only difference between me and a messenger boy was that I was taking a taxi instead of the subway.

Anyhow Wolfe had taken the job and there I was. I pulled a slip of paper from my pocket, typed on by me from notes taken of the talk with Harry Koven, and gave it a look.

8

MARCELLE KOVEN, wife
ADRIAN GETZ, friend or campfollower, maybe both
PATRICIA LOWELL, agent (manager?), promoter
PETE JORDAN, artist, draws Dazzle Dan
BYRAM HILDEBRAND, artist, also draws D.D.

One of those five, according to Harry Koven, had stolen his gun, a Marley .32, and he wanted to know which one. As he had told it, that was all there was to it, but it was a cinch that if the missing object had been an electric shaver or a pair of cuff links it would not have called for all that lip-chewing, not to mention other signs of strain. He had gone out of his way, not once but twice, to declare that he had no reason to suspect any of the five of wanting to do any shooting. The second time he had made it so emphatic that Wolfe had grunted and I had lifted a brow.

Since a Marley .32 is by no means a collector's item, it was no great coincidence that there was one in our arsenal and that therefore we were equipped to furnish Koven with the prop he wanted for his performance. As for the performance itself, the judicious thing to do was wait and see; but there was no point in being judicious about something I didn't like, so I had already checked it off as a dud.

I dismissed the taxi at the address on Seventy-sixth Street, east of Lexington Avenue. The house had had its front done over for the current century, unlike Nero Wolfe's old brownstone on West Thirty-fifth Street, which still sported the same front stoop it had started with. To enter this one you went down four steps instead of up seven, and I did so, after noting the pink shutters at the windows of all four floors and the tubs of evergreens flanking the entrance.

I was let in by a maid in uniform, with a pug nose and lipstick about as thick as Wolfe spreads Camembert on a wafer. I told her I had an appointment with Mr. Koven. She said Mr. Koven was not yet available and seemed to think that settled it, making me no offer for my hat and coat.

I said, "Our old brownstone, run by men only, is run better. When Fritz or I admit someone with an appointment we take his things."

"What's your name?" she demanded in a tone indicating that she doubted if I had one.

A loud male voice came from somewhere within. "Is that the man from Furnari's?"

A loud female voice came from up above. "Cora, is that my dress?"

I called out, "It's Archie Goodwin, expected by Mr. Koven at noon! It is now two minutes past twelve!"

That got action. The female voice, not quite so loud, told me to come up. The maid, looking frustrated, beat it. I took off my coat and put it on a chair, and my hat. A man came through a doorway at the rear of the hall and approached, speaking.

"More noise. Noisiest damn place. Up this way." He started up the stairs. "When you have an appointment with Sir Harry, always add an hour."

I followed him. At the top of the flight there was a large square hall with wide archways to rooms at right and left. He led me through the one at the left.

There are few rooms I can't take in at a glance, but that was one of them. Two huge TV cabinets, a monkey in a cage in a corner, chairs of all sizes and colors, rugs overlapping, a fireplace blazing away, the temperature around eighty—I gave it up and focused on the inhabitant. That was not only simpler but pleasanter. She was smaller than I would specify by choice, but otherwise acceptable, especially the wide smooth brow above the serious gray eyes, and the cheekbones. She must have been part salamander, to look so cool and silky in that oven.

"Dearest Pete," she said, "you are going to stop calling my husband Sir Harry."

I admired that as a timesaver. Instead of the usual pronouncement of names, she let me know that she was Marcelle, Mrs. Harry Koven, and that the young man was Pete Jordan, and at the same time told him something.

Pete Jordan walked across to her as for a purpose. He might have been going to take her in his arms or slap her or anything in between. But a pace short of her he stopped.

"You're wrong," he told her in his aggressive baritone.

"It's according to plan. It's the only way I can prove I'm not a louse. No one but a louse would stick at this, doing this junk month after month, and here look at me just because I like to eat. I haven't got the guts to quit and starve a while, so I call him Sir Harry to make you sore, working myself up to calling him something that will make *him* sore, and eventually I'll come to a boil and figure out a way to make Getz sore, and then I'll get bounced and I can start starving and be an artist. It's a plan."

He turned and glared at me. "I'm more apt to go through with it if I announce it in front of a witness. You're the witness. My name's Pete Jordan."

He shouldn't have tried glaring because he wasn't built for it. He wasn't much bigger than Mrs. Koven, and he had narrow shoulders and broad hips. An aggressive baritone and a defiant glare coming from that make-up just couldn't have the effect he was after. He needed coaching.

"You have already made me sore," she told his back in a nice low voice, but not a weak one. "You act like a brat and you're too old to be a brat. Why not grow up?"

He wheeled and snapped at her, "I look on you as a mother!"

That was a foul. They were both younger than me, and she couldn't have had more than three or four years on him.

I spoke. "Excuse me," I said, "but I am not a professional witness. I came to see Mr. Koven at his request. Shall I go hunt for him?"

A thin squeak came from behind me. "Good morning, Mrs. Koven. Am I early?"

As she answered I turned for a look at the owner of the squeak, who was advancing from the archway. He should have traded voices with Pete Jordan. He had both the size and presence for a deep baritone, with a well-made head topped by a healthy mat of gray hair nearly white. Everything about him was impressive and masterful, including the way he carried himself, but the squeak spoiled it completely. It continued as he joined us.

"I heard Mr. Goodwin, and Pete left, so I thought—"

Mrs. Koven and Pete were both talking, too, and it didn't

11

seem worth the effort to sort it out, especially when the monkey decided to join in and started chattering. Also I could feel sweat coming on my forehead and neck, over-dressed as I was with a coat and vest, since Pete and the newcomer were in shirt sleeves. I couldn't follow their example without displaying my holster. They kept it up, including the monkey, ignoring me completely but inform-ing me incidentally that the squeaker was not Adrian Getz as I had first supposed, but Byram Hildebrand, Pete's co-worker in the grind of drawing Dazzle Dan.

It was all very informal and homey, but I was starting to sizzle and I crossed to the far side of the room and opened a window wide. I expected an immediate reaction but got none. Disappointed at that but relieved by the rush of fresh air, I filled my chest, used my handkerchief on the brow and neck, turned, saw that we had company.

Coming through the archway was a pink-cheeked crea-ture in a mink coat with a dark green slab of cork or some-thing perched on her brown hair at a cocky slant. With no one bothering to glance at her except me, she moved across toward the fireplace, slid the coat off onto a couch, display-ing a tricky plaid suit with an assortment of restrained colors, and said in a throaty voice that carried without being raised, "Rookaloo will be dead in an hour."

They were all shocked into silence except the monkey. Mrs. Koven looked around, saw the open window, and de-manded, "Who did that?"

"I did," I said manfully.

Byram Hildebrand strode to the window like a general in front of troops and pulled it shut. The monkey stopped talking and started to cough.

"Listen to him," Pete Jordan said. His baritone mellowed when he was pleased. "Pneumonia already! That's an idea! That's what I'll do when I work up to making Getz sore."

Three of them went to the cage to take a look at Rookaloo, not bothering to greet or thank her who had come just in time to save the monkey's life. She stepped to me, asking cordially, "You're Archie Goodwin? I'm Pat Lowell." She put out a hand, and I took it. She had talent as a handclasper and backed it up with a good straight look out of clear brown eyes. "I was going to phone you this morning to warn you that Mr. Koven is never ready on time for an appointment, but he arranged this himself so I didn't."

"Never again," I told her, "pass up an excuse for phoning me."

"I won't." She took her hand back and glanced at her wrist. "You're early anyway. He told us the conference would be at twelve thirty."

"I was to come at twelve."

"Oh." She was taking me in—nothing offensive, but she sure was rating me. "To talk with him first?"

I shrugged. "I guess so."

She nodded, frowning a little. "This is a new one on me. I've been his agent and manager for three years now, handling all his business, everything from endorsements of cough drops to putting Dazzle Dan on scooters, and this is the first time a thing like this has happened, him getting someone in for a conference without consulting me—and Nero Wolfe, no less! I understand it's about a tie-up of Nero Wolfe and Dazzle Dan, having Dan start a detective agency?"

I put that question mark there, though her inflection left it to me whether to call it a question or merely a statement. I was caught off guard, so it probably showed on my face—my glee at the prospect of telling Wolfe about a tie-up between him and Dazzle Dan.

"We'd better wait," I said discreetly, "and let Mr. Koven tell it. As I understand it, I'm only here as a technical adviser, representing Mr. Wolfe because he never goes out on business. Of course you would handle the busines end, and if that means you and I will have to have a lot of talks—"

I stopped because I had lost her. Her eyes were aimed past my left shoulder toward the archway, and their expression had suddenly and completely changed. They weren't exactly more alive or alert, but more concentrated. I turned, and there was Harry Koven crossing to us. His mop of black hair hadn't been combed, and he hadn't shaved. His big frame was enclosed in a red silk robe embroidered with yellow Dazzle Dans. A little guy in a dark blue suit was with him, at his elbow.

"Good morning, my little dazzlers!" Koven boomed.

"It seems cool in here," the little guy said in a gentle worried voice.

In some mysterious way the gentle little voice seemed to make more noise than the big boom. Certainly it was the gentle little voice that chopped off the return greetings from the dazzlers, but it could have been the combination of the two, the big man and the small one, that had so abruptly changed the atmosphere of the room. Before they had all been screwy perhaps, but all free and easy; now they were all tightened up. They even seemed to be tongue-tied, so I spoke.

"I opened a window," I said.

"Good heavens," the little guy mildly reproached me and trotted over to the monkey's cage. Mrs. Koven and Pete Jordan were in his path, and they hastily moved out of it, as if afraid of getting trampled, though he didn't look up to trampling anything bigger than a cricket. Not only was he too little and too old, but also he was vaguely deformed and trotted with a jerk.

Koven boomed at me, "So you got here! Don't mind the Squirt and his damn monkey. He loves that damn monkey. I call this the steam room." He let out a laugh. "How is it, Squirt, okay?"

"I think so, Harry. I hope so." The low gentle voice filled the room again.

"I hope so, too, or God help Goodwin." Koven turned on Byram Hildebrand. "Has seven twenty-eight come, By?"

"No," Hildebrand squeaked. "I phoned Furnari, and he said it would be right over."

"Late again. We may have to change. When it comes, do a revise on the third frame. Where Dan says, 'Not tonight, my dear,' make it, 'Not today, my dear.' Got it?"

"But we discussed that—"

"I know, but change it. We'll change seven twenty-nine to fit. Have you finished seven thirty-three?"

"No. It's only—"

"Then what are you doing up here?"

"Why, Goodwin came, and you said you wanted us at

twelve thirty—"

"I'll let you know when we're ready—sometime after lunch. Show me the revise on seven twenty-eight." Koven glanced around masterfully. "How is everybody? Blooming? See you all later. Come along, Goodwin, sorry you had to wait. Come with me."

He headed for the archway and I followed, across the hall and up the next flight of stairs. There the arrangement was different; instead of a big square hall there was a narrow corridor with four doors, all closed. He turned left, to the door at that end, opened it, held it for me to pass through, and shut it again. This room was an improvement in several ways: it was ten degrees cooler, it had no monkey, and the furniture left more room to move around. The most prominent item was a big old scarred desk over by a window. After inviting me to sit, Koven went to the desk and removed covers from dishes that were there on a tray.

"Breakfast," he said. "You had yours."

It wasn't a question, but I said yes to be sociable. He needed all the sociability he could get, from the looks of the tray. There was one dejected poached egg, one wavy thin piece of toast, three undersized prunes with about a teaspoonful of juice, a split of tonic water, and a glass. It was an awful sight. He waded into the prunes. When they were gone he poured the tonic water into the glass, took a sip, and demanded, "Did you bring it?"

"The gun? Sure."

"Let me see it."

"It's the one we showed you at the office." I moved to another chair, closer to him. "I'm supposed to check with you before we proceed. Is that the desk you kept your gun in?"

He nodded and swallowed a nibble of toast. "Here in this left-hand drawer, in the back."

"Loaded."

"Yes. I told you so."

"So you did. You also told us that you bought it two years ago in Montana, when you were there at a dude ranch, and brought it home with you and never bothered to get a license for it, and it's been there in the drawer right along. You saw it there a week or ten days ago, and last Friday you saw it was gone. You didn't want to call the cops for two reasons, because you have no license for it, and because you think it was taken by one of the five people whose names you gave—"

"I think it *may* have been."

"You didn't put it like that. However, skip it. You gave us the five names. By the way, was that Adrian Getz, the one you called Squirt?"

"Yes."

"Then they're all five here, and we can go ahead and get it over with. As I understand it, I am to put my gun there in the drawer where yours was, and you get them up here for a conference, with me present. You were to cook up something to account for me. Have you done that?"

He swallowed another nibble of toast and egg. Wolfe would have had that meal down in five seconds flat—or rather, he would have had it out the window. "I thought this might do," Koven said. "I can say that I'm considering a new stunt for Dan, have him start a detective agency, and I've called Nero Wolfe in for consultation, and he sent you up for a conference. We can discuss it a little, and I ask you to show us how a detective searches a room to give us an idea of the picture potential. You shouldn't start with the desk; start maybe with the shelves back of me. When you come to do the desk I'll push my chair back to be out of your way, and I'll have them right in front of me. When you open the drawer and take the gun out and they see it—"

"I thought you were going to do that."

"I know, that's what I said, but this is better because this way they'll be looking at the gun and you, and I'll be watching their faces. I'll have my eye right on them, and the one that took my gun, if one of them did it—when he or she suddenly sees you pull a gun out of the drawer that's exactly like it, it's going to show on his face, and I'm going to see it. We'll do it that way."

I admit it sounded better there on the spot than it had in Wolfe's office—and besides, he might really get what he wanted.

"It sounds all right," I conceded, "except for one thing. You'll be expecting a look of surprise, but what if there are five looks of surprise? At seeing me take a gun out of your desk—those who don't know you had a gun there."

"But they do know."

"All of them?"

"Certainly. I thought I told you that. Anyhow, they all know. Everybody knows everything around this place. They thought I ought to get rid of it, and now I wish I had. You understand, Goodwin, all there is to this—I just want to know where the damn thing is, I want to know who took it, and I'll handle it myself from there. I told Wolfe that."

"I know you did." I got up and went to his side of the desk, at his left, and pulled a drawer open. "In here?"

"Yes."

"The rear compartment?"

"Yes."

I reached to my holster for the Marley, broke it, removed the cartridges, and dropped them into my vest pocket, put the gun in the drawer, shut the drawer, and returned to my chair.

"Okay," I said, "get them up here. We can ad lib it all right without any rehearsing."

He looked at me. He opened the drawer for a peek at the gun, not touching it, and pushed the drawer to.

"I'm going to have to get my nerve up," he said, as if appealing to me. "I'm never much good until late afternoon."

I grunted. "What the hell. You told me to be here at noon and called the conference for twelve thirty."

"I know I did. I do things like that. And I've got to dress." Suddenly his voice went high in protest. "Don't try to rush me, understand?"

I was fed up, but had already invested a lot of time and a dollar for a taxi, so kept calm. "I know," I told him, "artists are temperamental. But I'll explain how Mr. Wolfe charges. He sets a fee, depending on the job, and if it takes more of my time than he thinks reasonable he adds an extra hundred dollars an hour. Keeping me here until late afternoon would be expensive. I could go and come back."

He didn't like that and said so, explaining why, the

idea being that with me there in the house it would be easier for him to get his nerve up and it might only take an hour or so. He got up and walked to the door and opened it, then turned and demanded, "Do you know how much I make an hour? More than a thousand an hour! I'll go get some clothes on."

He went, shutting the door.

My wrist watch said 1:17. My stomach agreed. I sat maybe ten minutes, then went to the phone on the desk, dialed, got Wolfe, and told him how it was. He told me to go out and get some lunch, naturally, and I said I would, but after hanging up I went back to my chair. If I went out, sure as hell Koven would get his nerve up in my absence, and by the time I got back he would have lost it again and have to start over. I explained the situation to my stomach, and it made a polite sound of protest, but I was the boss. I was glancing at my watch again and seeing 1:42 when the door opened and Mrs. Koven was with me.

When I stood, her serious gray eyes beneath the wide smooth brow were level with the knot in my four-in-hand. She said her husband had told her that I was staying for a conference at a later hour. I confirmed it. She said I ought to have something to eat. I agreed that it was not a bad notion.

"Won't you," she invited, "come down and have a sandwich with us? We don't do any cooking, we even have our breakfast sent in, but there are some sandwiches."

"I don't want to be rude," I told her, "but are they in the room with the monkey?"

"Oh, no." She stayed serious. "Wouldn't that be awful? Downstairs in the workroom. Come on, do."

I went downstairs with her.

In a large room at the rear on the ground floor the other four suspects were seated around a plain wooden table, dealing with the sandwiches. The room was a mess—drawing tables under fluorescent lights, open shelves crammed with papers, cans of all sizes, and miscellaneous objects, chairs scattered around, other shelves with books and portfolios, and tables with more stacks of papers. Messy as it was to the eye, it was even messier to the ear, for two radios were going full blast.

Marcelle Koven and I joined them at the lunch table, and I perked up at once. There was a basket of French bread and pumpernickel, paper platters piled with slices of ham, smoked turkey, sturgeon, and hot corned beef, a big slab of butter, mustard and other accessories, bottles of milk, a pot of steaming coffee, and a one-pound jar of fresh caviar. Seeing Pete Jordan spooning caviar onto a piece of bread crust, I got what he meant about liking to eat.

"Help yourself!" Pat Lowell yelled into my ear.

I reached for the bread with one hand and the corned beef with the other and yelled back, "Why doesn't someone turn them down or even off?"

She took a sip of coffee from a paper cup and shook her head. "One's By Hildebrand's and one's Pete Jordan's! They like different programs when they're working! They have to go for volume!"

It was a hell of a din, but the corned beef was wonderful and the bread must have been from Rusterman's, nor was there anything wrong with the turkey and sturgeon. Since the radio duel precluded table talk, I used my eyes for diversion and was impressed by Adrian Getz, whom Koven called the Squirt. He would break off a rectangle of bread crust, place a rectangle of sturgeon on it, arrange a mound of caviar on top, and pop it in. When it was down he would take three sips of coffee and then start over. He was doing that when Mrs. Koven and I arrived and he was still doing it when I was full and reaching for another paper napkin.

Eventually, though, he stopped. He pushed back his chair, left it, went over to a sink at the wall, held his fingers under the faucet, and dried them with his handkerchief. Then he trotted over to a radio and turned it off, and to the other one and turned that off. Then he trotted back to us and spoke apologetically.

"That was uncivil, I know."

No one contradicted him.

"It was only," he went on, "that I wanted to ask Mr. Goodwin something before going up for my nap." His eyes settled on me. "Did you know when you opened that window that sudden cold drafts are dangerous for tropical monkeys?"

His tone was more than mild, it was wistful. But something about him—I didn't know what and didn't ask for time to go into it—got my goat.

"Sure," I said cheerfully. "I was trying it out."

"That was thoughtless," he said, not complaining, just giving his modest opinion, and turned and trotted out of the room.

There was a strained silence. Pat Lowell reached for the pot to pour some coffee.

"Goodwin, God help you," Pete Jordan muttered.

"Why? Does he sting?"

"Don't ask me why, but watch your step. I think he's a kobold." He tossed his paper napkin onto the table. "Want to see an artist create? Come and look." He marched to one of the radios and turned it on, then to a drawing table and sat.

"I'll clean up," Pat Lowell offered.

Byram Hildebrand, who had not squeaked once that I heard, went and turned on the other radio before he took his place at another drawing table.

Mrs. Koven left us. I helped Pat Lowell clear up the lunch table, but all that did was pass time, since both radios were going and I rely mostly on talk to develop an acquaintance in the early stages. Then she left, and I strolled over to watch the artists. So far nothing had occurred to change my opinion of Dazzle Dan, but I had to admire the way they did him. Working from rough sketches which all looked alike to me, they turned out the finished product in three colors so fast I could barely keep up, walking back and forth. The only interruptions for a long stretch were when Hildebrand jumped up to go and turn his radio louder, and a minute later Pete Jordan did likewise. I sat down and concentrated on the experiment of listening to two stations at once, but after a while my brain started to curdle and I got out of there.

A door toward the front of the lower hall was standing open, and I stepped inside when I saw Pat Lowell at a desk, working. She looked up to nod and went on working.

"Listen a minute," I said. "We're here on a desert island,

20

and for months you have been holding me at arm's length, and I'm desperate. It is not mere propinquity. In rags and tatters as you are, without make-up, I have come to look upon you—"

"I'm busy," she said emphatically. "Go play with a coconut."

"You'll regret this," I said savagely and went to the hall and looked through the glass of the front door at the outside world. The view was nothing to brag about, and the radios were still at my eardrums, so I went upstairs. Looking through the archway into the room at the left, and seeing no one but the monkey in its cage, I crossed to the other room and entered. It was full of furniture, but there was no sign of life. As I went up the second flight of stairs it seemed that the sound of the radios was getting louder instead of softer, and at the top I knew why. A radio was going on the other side of one of the closed doors.

I went and opened the door to the room where I had talked with Koven; not there. I tried another door and was faced by shelves stacked with linen. I knocked on another, got no response, opened it, and stepped in. It was a large bedroom, very fancy, with an over-sized bed. The furniture and fittings showed that it was co-ed. A radio on a stand was giving with a soap opera, and stretched out on a couch was Mrs. Koven, sound asleep. She looked softer and not so serious, with her lips parted a little and relaxed fingers curled on the cushion, in spite of the yapping radio on the bedside table.

I damn well intended to find Koven, and took a couple of steps with a vague notion of looking under the bed for him, when a glance through an open door at the right into the next room discovered him. He was standing at a window with his back to me. Thinking it might seem a little familiar on short acquaintance for me to enter from the bedroom where his wife was snoozing, I backed out to the hall, pulling the door to, moved to the next door, and knocked. Getting no reaction, I turned the knob and entered.

The radio had drowned out my noise. He remained at the window. I banged the door shut. He jerked around. He said something, but I didn't get it on account of the radio. I went and closed the door to the bedroom, and that helped some.

"Well?" he demanded, as if he couldn't imagine who I was or what I wanted.

He had shaved and combed and had on a well-made brown homespun suit, with a tan shirt and red tie.

"It's going on four o'clock," I said, "and I'll be going soon and taking my gun with me."

He took his hands from his pockets and dropped into a chair. Evidently this was the Koven personal living room, from the way it was furnished, and it looked fairly livable.

He spoke. "I was standing at the window thinking."

"Yeah. Any luck?"

He sighed and stretched his legs out. "Fame and fortune," he said, "are not all a man needs for happiness."

"What else would you suggest?" I asked brightly.

He undertook to tell me. He went on and on, but I won't report it verbatim because I doubt if it contained any helpful hints for you—I know it didn't for me. I grunted from time to time to be polite. I listened to him for a while and then got a little relief by listening to the soap opera on the radio, which was muffled some by the closed door but by no means inaudible. Eventually, of course, he got around to his wife, first briefing me by explaining that she was his third and they had been married only two years. To my surprise he didn't tear her apart. He said she was wonderful. His point was that even when you added to fame and fortune the companionship of a beloved and loving wife who was fourteen years younger than you, that still wasn't all you needed for happiness.

There was one interruption—a knock on the door and the appearance of Byram Hildebrand. He had come to show the revise on the third frame of Number 728. They discussed art some, and Koven okayed the revise, and Hildebrand departed. I hoped that the intermission had sidetracked Koven, but no; he took up again where he had left off.

I can take a lot when I'm working on a case, even a kindergarten problem like that one, but finally, after the twentieth sidewise glance at my wrist, I called a halt.

"Look," I said, "this has given me a new slant on life,

and don't think I don't appreciate it, but it's a quarter past four and it's getting dark. I would call it late afternoon. What do you say we go ahead with our act?"

He closed his trap and frowned at me. He started chewing his lip. After some of that he suddenly arose, went to a cabinet, and got out a bottle.

"Will you join me?" He produced two glasses. "I'm not supposed to drink until five o'clock, but I'll make this an exception." He came to me. "Bourbon all right? Say when."

I would have liked to plug him. He had known from the beginning that he would have to drink himself up to it but had sucked me in with a noon appointment. Anything I felt like saying would have been justified, but I held it in. I accepted mine and raised it with him, to encourage him, and took a swallow. He took a dainty sip, raised his eyes to the ceiling, then emptied the glass at a gulp. He picked up the bottle and poured a refill.

"Why don't we go in there with the refreshment," I suggested, "and go over it a little?"

"Don't rush me," he said gloomily. He took a deep breath, swelling his chest, and suddenly grinned at me, showing the teeth. He lifted the glass and drained it, reached for the bottle and tilted it to pour, and changed his mind.

"Come on," he said, heading for the door. I stepped around him to open the door, since both his hands were occupied, closed it behind us, and followed him down the hall. At the farther end we entered the room where we were to stage it. He went to the desk and sat, poured himself a drink, and put the bottle down. I went to the desk, too, but not to sit. I had taken the precaution of removing the cartridges from my gun, but even so a glance at it wouldn't hurt any. I pulled the drawer open and was relieved to see that it was still there. I shut the drawer.

"I'll go get them," I offered.

"I said don't rush me," Koven protested, but no longer gloomy.

Thinking that two more drinks would surely do it, I moved to a chair. But I didn't sit. Something wasn't right, and it came to me what it was: I had placed the gun with the muzzle pointing to the right, and it wasn't that way now. I returned to the desk, took the gun out, and gave it a look.

It was a Marley .32 all right—but not mine.

I put my eye on Koven. The gun was in my left hand, and my right hand was a fist. If I had hit him that first second, which I nearly did, mad as I was, I would have cracked some knuckles.

"What's the matter?" he demanded.

My eyes were on him and through him. I kept them there for five pulse beats. It wasn't possible, I decided, that he was that good. Nobody could be.

I backed up a pace. "We've found your gun."

He gawked at me. "What?"

I broke it, saw that the cylinder was empty, and held it out. "Take a look."

He took it. "It looks the same—no, it doesn't."

"Certainly it doesn't. Mine was clean and bright. Is it yours?"

"I don't know. It looks like it. But how in the name of—"

I reached and took it from him. "How do you think? Someone with hands took mine out and put yours in. It could have been you. Was it?"

"No. Me?" Suddenly he got indignant. "How the hell could it have been me when I didn't know where mine was?"

"You said you didn't. I ought to stretch you out and tamp you down. Keeping me here the whole damn day, and now this! If you ever talk straight and to the point, now is the time. Did you touch my gun?"

"No. But you're—"

"Do you know who did?"

"No. But you're—"

"Shut up!" I went around the desk to the phone, lifted it, and dialed. At that hour Wolfe would be up in the plant rooms for his afternoon shift with the orchids, where he was not to be disturbed except in emergency, but this was one. When Fritz answered I asked him to buzz the extension, and in a moment I had Wolfe.

"Yes, Archie?" Naturally he was peevish.

"Sorry to bother you, but I'm at Koven's. I put my gun in his desk, and we were all set for his stunt, but he kept putting it off until now. His will power sticks and has to be primed with alcohol. I roamed around. We just came in here where his desk is, and I opened the drawer for a look. Someone has taken my gun and substituted his—his that was stolen, you know? It's back where it belongs, but mine is gone."

"You shouldn't have left it there."

"Okay, but I need instructions for now. Three choices: I can call a cop, or I can bring the whole bunch down there to you, or I can handle it myself. Which?"

"Confound it, not the police. They would enjoy it too much. And why bring them here? The gun's there, not here."

"Then that leaves me. I go ahead?"

"Certainly—with due discretion. It's a prank." He chuckled. "I would like to see your face. Try to get home for dinner." He hung up.

"My God, don't call a cop!" Koven protested.

"I don't intend to," I said grimly. I slipped his gun into my armpit holster. "Not if I can help it. It depends partly on you. You stay put, right here. I'm going down and get them. Your wife's asleep in the bedroom. If I find when I get back that you've gone and started chatting with her I'll either slap you down with your own gun or phone the police, I don't know which, maybe both. Stay put."

"This is my house, Goodwin, and—"

"Damn it, don't you know a raving maniac when you see one?" I tapped my chest with a forefinger. "Me. When I'm as sore as I am now the safest thing would be for *you* to call a cop. I want my gun."

As I made for the door he was reaching for the bottle. By the time I got down to the ground floor I had myself well enough in hand to speak to them without betraying any special urgency, telling them that Koven was ready for them upstairs, for the conference. I found Pat Lowell still at the desk in the room in front and Hildebrand and Jordan still at their drawing tables in the workroom. I even replied appropriately when Pat Lowell asked how I had made out with the coconut. As Hildebrand and Jordan left their tables and turned off their radios I had a keener eye on them than before; someone here had swiped my gun. As we ascended the first flight of stairs, with me in the rear, I asked their backs where I would find Adrian Getz.

Pat Lowell answered. "He may be in his room on the top floor." They halted at the landing, the edge of the big square hall, and I joined them. We could hear the radio going upstairs. She indicated the room to the left. "He takes his afternoon nap in there with Rookaloo, but not this late usually."

I thought I might as well glance in, and moved to the archway. A draft of cold air hit me, and I went on in. A window was wide open! I marched over and closed it, then went to take a look at the monkey. It was huddled on the floor in a corner of the cage, making angry little noises, with something clutched in its fingers against its chest. The light was dim, but I have good eyes, and not only was the something unmistakably a gun, but it was my Marley on a bet. Needing light, and looking for a wall switch, I was passing the large couch which faced the fireplace when suddenly I stopped and froze.

Adrian Getz, the Squirt, was lying on the couch but he wasn't taking a nap.

I bent over him for a close-up and saw a hole in his skull northeast of his right ear, and some red juice. I stuck a hand inside the V of his vest and flattened it against him and held my breath for eight seconds. He was through taking naps.

I straightened up and called, "Come in here, all three of you, and switch on a light as you come!"

They appeared through the archway, and one of them put a hand to the wall. Lights shone. The back of the couch hid Getz from their view as they approached.

"It's cold in here," Pat Lowell was saying. "Did you open another—"

Seeing Getz stopped her, and the others, too. They goggled.

"Don't touch him," I warned them. "He's dead, so you can't help him any. Don't touch anything. You three stay

26

here together, right here in this room, while I—"

"God Almighty," Pete Jordan blurted. Hildebrand squeaked something. Pat Lowell put out a hand, found the couch back, and gripped it. She asked something, but I wasn't listening. I was at the cage, with my back to them, peering at the monkey. It was my Marley the monkey was clutching. I had to curl my fingers until the nails sank in to keep from opening the cage door and grabbing that gun.

I whirled. "Stick here together. Understand?" I was on my way. "I'm going up and phone."

Ignoring their noises, I left them. I mounted the stairs in no hurry, because if I had been a raving maniac before, I was now stiff with fury and I needed a few seconds to get under control. In the room upstairs Harry Koven was still seated at the desk, staring at the open drawer. He looked up and fired a question at me but got no answer. I went to the phone, lifted it, and dialed a number. When I got Wolfe he started to sputter at being disturbed again.

"I'm sorry," I told him, "but I wish to report that I have found my gun. It's in the cage with the monkey, who is—"

"What monkey?"

"Its name is Rookaloo, but please don't interrupt. It is holding my gun to its breast, I suspect because it is cold and the gun is warm, having recently been fired. Lying there on a couch is the body of a man, Adrian Getz, with a bullet hole in the head. It is no longer a question whether I call a cop, I merely wanted to report the situation to you before I do so. A thousand to one Getz was shot and killed with my gun. I will not be—hold it—"

I dropped the phone and jumped. Koven had made a dive for the door. I caught him before he reached it, got an arm and his chin, and heaved. There was a lot of feeling in it, and big as he was he sailed to a wall, bounced off, and went to the floor.

"I would love to do it again," I said, meaning it, and returned to the phone and told Wolfe, "Excuse me, Koven tried to interrupt. I was going to say I will not be home to dinner."

"The man is dead."

"Yes, sir."

"Have you anything satisfactory for the police?"

"Sure. My apologies for bringing my gun here to oblige a murderer. That's all."

"We haven't answered today's mail."

"I know. It's a damn shame. I'll get away as soon as I can."

"Very well."

The connection went. I held the button down a moment, with an eye on Koven, who was upright again but not asking for an encore, then released it and dialed the police.

I haven't kept anything like an accurate score, but I would say that over the years I haven't told the cops more than a couple of dozen barefaced lies, maybe not that many. They are seldom practical. On the other hand, I can't recall any murder case Wolfe and I were in on and I've had my story gone into at length where I have simply opened the bag and given them all I had, with no dodging and no withholding, except one, and this is it. On the murder of Adrian Getz I didn't have a single thing on my mind that I wasn't willing and eager to shovel out, so I let them have it.

It worked fine. They called me a liar.

Not right away, of course. At first even Inspector Cramer appreciated my cooperation, knowing as he did that there wasn't a man in his army who could shade me at seeing and hearing, remembering and reporting. It was generously conceded that on finding the body I had performed properly and promptly, herding the trio into the room and keeping the Kovens from holding a family council until the law arrived. From there on, of course, everyone had been under surveillance, including me.

At six thirty, when the scientists were still monopolizing the room where Getz had got it, and city employees were wandering all over the place, and the various inmates were still in various rooms, conversing privately with Homicide men, and I had typed and signed my own frank and full statement, I was confidently expecting that I would soon be out on the sidewalk unattended, flagging a taxi. I was in the front room on the ground floor, seated at Pat Lowell's desk, having used her typewriter, and Sergeant Purley Stebbins was sitting across from me, looking over my statement.

He lifted his head and regarded me, perfectly friendly. A perfectly friendly look from Stebbins would, from almost anyone else, cause you to get your guard up and be ready to either duck or counter, but Purley wasn't responsible for the design of his big bony face and his pig-bristle eyebrows.

"I guess you got it all in," he admitted. "As you told it."

"I suggest," I said modestly, "that when this case is put away you send that to the school to be used as a model report."

"Yeah." He stood up. "You're a good typist." He turned to go.

I arose, too, saying casually, "I can run along now?"

The door opened and Inspector Cramer entered. I didn't like his expression as he darted a glance at me. Knowing him well in all his moods, I didn't like the way his broad shoulders were hunched, or his clamped jaw, or the glint in his eye.

"Here's Goodwin's statement," Purley said. "Okay?"

"Send him downtown and hold him."

It caught me completely off balance. "Hold *me?*" I demanded, squeaking almost like Hildebrand.

"Yes, sir." Nothing could catch Purley off balance. "On your order?"

"No, charge him. Sullivan Act. He has no license for the gun we found on him."

"Ha, ha," I said. "Ha, ha, and ha, ha. There, you got your laugh. A very fine gag. Ha."

"You're going down, Goodwin. I'll be down to see you later."

As I said, I knew him well. He meant it. I had his eyes. "This," I said, "is way out of my reach. I've told you where and how and why I got that gun." I pointed to the paper in Purley's hand. "Read it. It's all down, punctuated."

"Nuts. But I get it. You've been hoping for years to hang something on Nero Wolfe, and to you I'm just a part of him, and you think here's your chance. Of course it won't stick. Wouldn't you rather have something that will? Like

29

resisting arrest and assaulting an officer? Glad to oblige. Watch it—"

Tipping forward, I started a left hook for his jaw, fast and vicious, then jerked it down and went back on my heels. It didn't create a panic, but I had the satisfaction of seeing Cramer take a quick step back and Stebbins one forward. They bumped.

"There," I said. "With both of you to swear to it, that ought to be good for at least two years. I'll throw the typewriter at you if you'll promise to catch it."

"Cut the clowning," Purley growled.

"You lied about that gun," Cramer snapped. "If you don't want to get taken down to think it over, think now. Tell me what you came here for and what happened."

"I've told you."

"A string of lies."

"No, sir."

"You can have 'em back. I'm not trying to hang something on Wolfe, or you either. I want to know why you came here and what happened."

"Oh, for God's sake." I moved my eyes. "Okay, Purley, where's my escort?"

Cramer strode four paces to the door, opened it, and called, "Bring Mr. Koven in here!"

Harry Koven entered with a dick at his elbow. He looked as if he was even farther away from happiness than before.

"We'll sit down," Cramer said.

He left me behind the desk. Purley and the dick took chairs in the background. Cramer stationed himself across the desk from me, where Purley had been, with Koven on a chair at his left. He opened up.

"I told you, Mr. Koven, that I would ask you to repeat your story in Goodwin's presence, and you said you would."

Koven nodded. "That's right." He was hoarse.

"We won't need all the details. Just answer me briefly. When you called on Nero Wolfe last Saturday evening, what did you ask him to do?"

"I told him I was going to have Dazzle Dan start a detective agency in a new series. I told him I needed technical assistance, and possibly a tie-up, if we could arrange—"

There was a pad of ruled paper on the desk. I reached for it, and a pencil, and started doing shorthand. Cramer leaned over, stretched an arm, grabbed a corner of the pad, and jerked it away.

"We need your full attention," Cramer growled. He went to Koven. "Did you say anything to Wolfe about your gun being taken from your desk?"

"Certainly not. It hadn't been taken. I did mention that I had a gun in my desk for which I had no license, but that I never carried it, and I asked if that was risky. I told them what make it was, a Marley .32. I asked how much trouble it would be to get a license, and if—"

"Keep it brief. Just cover the points. What arrangement did you make with Wolfe?"

"He agreed to send Goodwin to my place on Monday for a conference with my staff and me."

"About what?"

"About the technical problems of having Dazzle Dan do detective work, and possibly a tie-up."

"And Goodwin came?"

"Yes, today around noon." Koven's hoarseness kept interfering with him, and he kept clearing his throat. My eyes were at his face, but he hadn't met them. Of course he was talking to Cramer and had to be polite. He went on, "The conference was for twelve thirty, but I had a little talk with Goodwin and asked him to wait. I have to be careful what I do with Dan and I wanted to think it over some more. Anyway, I'm like that, I put things off. It was after four o'clock when he—"

"Was your talk with Goodwin about your gun being gone?"

"Certainly not. We might have mentioned the gun, about my not having a license for it, I don't remember—no, wait a minute, we must have, because I pulled the drawer open and we glanced in at it. Except for that, we only talked—"

"Did you or Goodwin take your gun out of the drawer?"

"No. Absolutely not."

"Did he put his gun in the drawer?"

"Absolutely not."

I slid in, "When I took my gun from my holster to show

it to you, did you—"

"Nothing doing," Cramer snapped at me. "You're listening. Just the high spots for now." He returned to Koven. "Did you have another talk with Goodwin later?"

Koven nodded. "Yes, around half-past three he came up to my room—the living room. We talked until after four, there and in my office, and then—"

"In your office did Goodwin open the drawer of the desk and take the gun out and say it had been changed?"

"Certainly not!"

"What did he do?"

"Nothing, only we talked, and then he left to go down and get the others to come up for the conference. After a while he came back alone, and without saying anything he came to the desk and took my gun from the drawer and put it under his coat. Then he went to the phone and called Nero Wolfe. When I heard him tell Wolfe that Adrian Getz had been shot, that he was on a couch downstairs dead, I got up to go down there, and Goodwin jumped me from behind and knocked me out. When I came to he was still talking to Wolfe, I don't know what he was telling him, and then he called the police. He wouldn't let me—"

"Hold it," Cramer said curtly. "That covers that. One more point. Do you know of any motive for Goodwin's wanting to murder Adrian Getz?"

"No, I don't. I told—"

"Then if Getz was shot with Goodwin's gun how would you account for it? You're not obliged to account for it, but if you don't mind just repeat what you told me."

"Well—" Koven hesitated. He cleared his throat for the twentieth time. "I told you about the monkey. Goodwin opened a window, and that's enough to kill that kind of monkey, and Getz was very fond of it. He didn't show how upset he was but Getz was very quiet and didn't show things much. I understand Goodwin likes to kid people. Of course I don't know what happened, but if Goodwin went in there later when Getz was there, and started to open a window, you can't tell. When Getz once got aroused he was apt to do anything. He couldn't have hurt Goodwin any, but Goodwin might have got out his gun just for a gag, and

Getz tried to take it away, and it went off accidentally. That wouldn't be murder, would it?"

"No," Cramer said, "that would only be regrettable accident. That's all for now, Mr. Koven. Take him out, Sol, and bring Hildebrand."

As Koven arose and the dick came forward I reached for the phone on Pat Lowell's desk. My hand got there, but so did Cramer's, hard on top of mine.

"The lines here are busy," he stated. "There'll be a phone you can use downtown. Do you want to hear Hildebrand before you comment?"

"I'm crazy to hear Hildebrand," I assured him. "No doubt he'll explain that I tossed the gun in the monkey's cage to frame the monkey. Let's just wait for Hildebrand."

It wasn't much of a wait; the Homicide boys are snappy. Byram Hildebrand, ushered in by Sol, gave me a long straight look before he took the chair Koven had vacated. He still had good presence, with his fine mat of nearly white hair, but his extremities were nervous. When he sat he couldn't find comfortable spots for either his hands or his feet.

"This will only take a minute," Cramer told him. "I just want to check on Sunday morning. Yesterday. You were here working?"

Hildebrand nodded, and the squeak came. "I was putting on some touches. I often work Sundays."

"You were in there in the workroom?"

"Yes. Mr. Getz was there, making some suggestions. I was doubtful about one of his suggestions and went upstairs to consult Mr. Koven, but Mrs. Koven was in the hall and—"

"You mean the big hall one flight up?"

"Yes. She said Mr. Koven wasn't up yet and Miss Lowell was in his office waiting to see him. Miss Lowell has extremely good judgment, and I went up to consult her. She disapproved of Mr. Getz's suggestion, and we discussed various matters, and mention was made of the gun Mr. Koven kept in his desk drawer. I pulled the drawer open just to look at it, with no special purpose, merely to look at it, and closed the drawer again. Shortly afterward I returned downstairs."

"Was the gun there in the drawer?"

"Yes."

"Did you take it out?"

"No. Neither did Miss Lowell. We didn't touch it."

"But you recognized it as the same gun?"

"I can't say that I did, no. I had never examined the gun, never had it in my hand. I can only say that it looked the same as before. It was my opinion that our concern about the gun being kept there was quite childish, but I see now that I was wrong. After what happened today—"

"Yeah." Cramer cut him off. "Concern about a loaded gun is never childish. That's all I'm after now. Okay, that's all." Cramer nodded at Sol. "Take him back to Rowcliff."

I treated myself to a good deep breath. Purley was squinting at me, not gloating, just concentrating. Cramer turned his head to see that the door was closed after the dick and the artist, then turned back to me.

"Your turn," he growled.

I shook my head. "Lost my voice," I whispered.

"You're not funny, Goodwin. You're never as funny as you think you are. This time you're not funny at all. You can have five minutes to go over it and realize how complicated it is. When you phoned Wolfe *before* you phoned us, you couldn't possibly have arranged all the details. I've got you. I'll be leaving here before long to join you downtown and on my way I'll stop in at Wolfe's for a talk. He won't clam up in this one. At the very least I've got you good on the Sullivan Act. Want five minutes?"

"No, sir." I was calm but emphatic. "I want five days and I would advise you to take a full week. Complicated doesn't begin to describe it. Before I leave for downtown, if you're actually going to crawl out on that one, I wish to remind you of something, and don't forget it. When I voluntarily took Koven's gun from my holster and turned it over—it wasn't 'found on me,' as you put it—I also turned over six nice clean cartridges which I had in my vest pocket, having previously removed them from my gun. I hope none of your heroes gets careless and mixes them up with the cartridges found in my gun, if any, when you retrieved it from the monkey. That would be a mistake. The point is, if I removed the cartridges from my gun in order to insert one or more from Koven's gun, when and why did I do it? There's a day's work for you right there. And if I did do it, then Koven's friendly effort to fix me up for justifiable manslaughter is wasted, much as I appreciate it, because I must have been premeditating something, and you know what. Why fiddle around with the Sullivan Act? Make it the big one. Now I button up."

Cramer eyed me. "Even a suspended sentence," he said, "you lose your license."

I grinned at him.

"Send him down," Cramer rasped.

Even when a man is caught smack in the middle of a felony, as I had been, there is a certain amount of red tape to getting him behind bars, and in my case not only red tape but also other activities postponed my attainment of privacy. First, I had a long conversation with an Assistant District Attorney, who was the suave and subtle type and even ate sandwiches with me. When it was over, a little after nine o'clock, both of us were only slightly more confused than when we started. He left me in a room with a specimen in uniform with slick brown hair and a wart on his cheek. I told him how to get rid of the wart, recommending Doc Vollmer.

I was expecting the promised visit by Inspector Cramer any minute. Naturally I was nursing an assorted collection of resentments, but the one on top was at not being there to see and hear the talk between Cramer and Wolfe. Any chat those two had was always worth listening to, and that one must have been outstanding, with Wolfe learning not only that his client was lying five ways from Sunday, which was bad enough, but also that I had been tossed in the can and the day's mail would have to go unanswered.

When the door finally opened and a visitor entered it wasn't Inspector Cramer. It was Lieutenant Rowcliff, whose murder I will not have to premeditate when I get around to it because I have already done the premeditating. There are not many murderers so vicious and inhuman that I would enjoy seeing them caught by Rowcliff. He jerked a chair around to sit facing me and said with oily satisfaction, "At last we've got you."

That set the tone of the interview.

I would enjoy recording in full that two-hour session with Rowcliff, but it would sound like bragging, and therefore I don't suppose you would enjoy it, too. His biggest handicap is that when he gets irritated to a certain point he can't help stuttering, and I'm onto him enough to tell when he's just about there, and then I start stuttering before he does. Even with a close watch and careful timing it takes luck to do it right, and that evening I was lucky. He came closer than ever before to plugging me, but didn't, because he wants to be a captain so bad he can taste it and he's not absolutely sure that Wolfe hasn't got a solid in with the Commissioner or even the Mayor.

Cramer never showed up, and that added another resentment to my healthy pile. I knew he had been to see Wolfe, because when they had finally let me make my phone call, around eight o'clock, and I had got Wolfe and started to tell him about it, he interrupted me in a voice as cold as an Eskimo's nose.

"I know where you are and how you got there. Mr. Cramer is here. I have phoned Mr. Parker, but it's too late to do anything tonight. Have you had anything to eat?"

"No, sir. I'm afraid of poison and I'm on a hunger strike."

"You should eat something. Mr. Cramer is worse than a jackass, he's demented. I intend to persuade him, if possible, of the desirability of releasing you at once."

He hung up.

When, shortly after eleven, Rowcliff called it off and I was shown to my room, there had been no sign of Cramer. The room was in no way remarkable, merely what was to be expected in a structure of that type; but it was fairly clean, strongly scented with disinfectant, and was in a favorable location since the nearest corridor light was six paces away and therefore did not glare through the bars of my door. Also it was a single, which I appreciated. Alone at last, away from telephones and other interruptions, I undressed and arranged my gray pinstripe on the chair, draped my shirt over the end of the blankets, got in, stretched, and settled down for a complete survey of the complications. But my brain and nerves had other plans, and in twenty seconds I was asleep.

In the morning there was a certain amount of activity, with the check-off and a trip to the lavatory and breakfast, but after that I had more privacy than I really cared for. By noon I would almost have welcomed a visit from Rowcliff and was beginning to suspect that someone had lost a paper and there was no record of me anywhere and everyone was too busy to stop and think. Lunch, which I will not describe, broke the monotony some, but then, back in my room, I decided to spread all the pieces out, sort them, and have a look at the picture as it had been drawn to date; but it got so damn jumbled that I couldn't make first base, let alone on around.

At 1:09 my door swung open and the floorwalker, a chunky short guy with only half an ear on the right side, told me to come along. I went willingly, on out of the block to an elevator, and along a ground-floor corridor to an office. There I was pleased to see the tall lanky figure and long pale face of Henry George Parker, the only lawyer Wolfe would admit to the bar if he had the say. He came to shake my hand and said he'd have me out of there in a minute now.

"No rush," I said stiffly. "Don't let it interfere with anything important."

He laughed, haw-haw, and took me inside the gate. All the formalities but one which required my presence had already been attended to, and he made good on his minute. On the way up in the taxi he explained why I had been left to rot until past noon. Getting bail on the Sullivan Act charge had been simple, but I had also been tagged with a material witness warrant, and the D.A. had asked the judge to put it at fifty grand! He had been stubborn about it, and the best Parker could do was talk it down to twenty, and he had had to report back to Wolfe before closing the deal. I was not to leave the jurisdiction. As the taxi crossed Thirty-fourth Street I looked west across the river. I had never cared much for New Jersey, but now the idea of driving through the tunnel and on among the billboards seemed attractive.

I preceded Parker up the stoop at the old brownstone on West Thirty-fifth, used my key but found that the chain bolt was on, which was normal but not invariable when I was out of the house, and had to push the button. Fritz Brenner, chef and house manager, let us in and stood while we disposed of our coats and hats.

"Are you all right, Archie?" he inquired.

"No," I said frankly. "Don't you smell me?"

As we went down the hall Wolfe appeared, coming from the door to the dining room. He stopped and regarded me. I returned his gaze with my chin up.

"I'll go up and rinse off," I said, "while you're finishing lunch."

"I've finished," he said grimly. "Have you eaten?"

"Enough to hold me."

"Then we'll get started."

He marched into the office, across the hall from the dining room, went to his oversized chair behind his desk, sat, and got himself adjusted for comfort. Parker took the red leather chair. As I crossed to my desk I started talking, to get the jump on him.

"It will help," I said, not aggressively but pointedly, "if we first get it settled about my leaving that room with my gun there in the drawer. I do not—"

"Shut up!" Wolfe snapped.

"In that case," I demanded, "why didn't you leave me in the coop? I'll go back and—"

"Sit down!"

I sat.

"I deny," he said, "that you were in the slightest degree imprudent. Even if you were, this has transcended such petty considerations." He picked up a sheet of paper from his desk. "This is a letter which came yesterday from a Mrs. E. R. Baumgarten. She wants me to investigate the activities of a nephew who is employed by the business she owns. I wish to reply. Your notebook."

He was using what I call his conclusive tone, leaving no room for questions, let alone argument. I got my notebook and pen.

"Dear Mrs. Baumgarten." He went at it as if he had already composed it in his mind. "Thank you very much for your letter of the thirteenth, requesting me to undertake an investigation for you. Paragraph. I am sorry that I cannot be of service to you. I am compelled to decline because I have been informed by an official of the New York Police Department that my license to operate a private detective agency is about to be taken away from me. Sincerely yours."

Parker ejaculated something and got ignored. I stayed deadpan, but among my emotions was renewed regret that I had missed Wolfe's and Cramer's talk.

Wolfe was saying, "Type it at once and send Fritz to mail it. If any requests for appointments come by telephone refuse them, giving the reason and keeping a record."

"The reason given in the letter?"

"Yes."

I swiveled the typewriter to me, got paper and carbon in, and hit the keys. I had to concentrate. Parker was asking questions, and Wolfe was grunting at him. I finished the letter and envelope, had Wolfe sign it, went to the kitchen and told Fritz to take it to Eighth Avenue immediately, and returned to the office.

"Now," Wolfe said, "I want all of it. Go ahead."

Ordinarily when I start giving Wolfe a full report of an event, no matter how extended and involved, I just glide in and keep going with no effort at all, thanks to my long and hard training. That time, having just got a severe jolt, I wasn't so hot at the beginning, since I was supposed to include every word and movement, but by the time I had got to where I opened the window it was coming smooth and easy. As usual, Wolfe soaked it all in without making any interruptions.

It took all of an hour and a half, and then came questions, but not many. I rate a report by the number of questions he has when I'm through, and by that test this was up toward the top. Wolfe leaned back and closed his eyes.

Parker spoke. "It could have been any of them, but it

must have been Koven. Or why his string of lies, knowing that you and Goodwin would both contradict him?" The lawyer haw-hawed. "That is, if they're lies—considering your settled policy of telling your counselor only what you think he should know."

"Pfui." Wolfe's eyes came open. "This is extraordinarily intricate, Archie. Have you examined it any?"

"I've started. When I pick at it, it gets worse instead of better."

"Yes. I'm afraid you'll have to type it out. By eleven to-morrow morning?"

"I guess so, but I need a bath first. Anyway, what for? What can we do with it without a license? I suppose it's suspended?"

He ignored it. "What the devil is that smell?" he demanded.

"Disinfectant. It's for the bloodhounds in case you escape." I arose. "I'll go scrub."

"No." He glanced at the wall clock, which said 3:45—fifteen minutes to go until he was due to join Theodore and the orchids up on the roof. "An errand first. I believe it's the *Gazette* that carries the Dazzle Dan comic strip?"

"Yes, sir."

"Daily and Sunday?"

"Yes, sir."

"I want all of them for the past three years. Can you get them?"

"Now?"

"Yes. Wait on a minute—confound it, don't be a cyclone! You should hear my instructions for Mr. Parker, but first one for you. Mail Mr. Koven a bill for recovery of his gun—five hundred dollars. It should go today."

"Any extras, under the circumstances?"

"No. Five hundred flat." Wolfe turned to the lawyer. "Mr. Parker, how long will it take to enter a suit for damages and serve a summons on the defendant?"

"That depends." Parker sounded like a lawyer. "If it's rushed all possible and there are no unforeseen obstacles and the defendant is accessible for service, it could be merely a matter of hours."

"By noon tomorrow?"

"Quite possibly, yes."

"Then proceed, please. Mr. Koven has destroyed, by slander, my means of livelihood. I wish to bring an action demanding payment by him of the sum of one million dollars."

"M-m-m-m," Parker said. He was frowning.

I addressed Wolfe. "I want to apologize," I told him, "for jumping to a conclusion. I was supposing you had lost control for once and buried it too deep in Cramer. Whereas you did it purposely, getting set for this. I'll be damned."

Wolfe grunted.

"In this sort of thing," Parker said, "it is usual, and desirable, to first send a written request for recompense, by your attorney if you prefer. It looks better."

"I don't care how it looks. I want immediate action."

"Then we'll act." That was one of the reasons Wolfe stuck to Parker; he was no dilly-dallier. "But I must ask, isn't the sum a little flamboyant?"

"It is not flamboyant. At a hundred thousand a year, a modest expectation, my income would be a million in ten years. A detective license once lost in this fashion is not easily regained."

"All right. A million. I'll need all the facts for drafting a complaint."

"You have them. You've just heard Archie recount them. Must you stickle for more?"

"No. I'll manage." Parker got to his feet. "One thing, though, service of process may be a problem. Policemen may still be around, and even if they aren't I doubt if strangers will be getting into that house tomorrow."

"Archie will send Saul Panzer to you. Saul can get in anywhere and do anything." Wolfe wiggled a finger. "I want Mr. Koven to get that. I want to see him in this room. Five times this morning I tried to get him on the phone, without success. If that doesn't get him I'll devise something that will."

"He'll give it to his attorney."

"Then the attorney will come, and if he's not an imbecile I'll give myself thirty minutes to make him send for his client or go and get him. Well?"

Parker turned and left. I got at the typewriter to make out a bill for half a grand, which seemed like a waste of paper after what I had just heard.

At midnight that Tuesday the office was a sight. It has often been a mess, one way and another, including the time the strangled Cynthia Brown was lying on the floor with her tongue protruding, but this was something new. Dazzle Dan, both black-and-white and color, was all over the place. On account of our shortage in manpower, with me tied up on my typing job, Fritz and Theodore had been drafted for the chore of tearing out the pages and stacking them chronologically, ready for Wolfe to study. With Wolfe's permission, I had bribed Lon Cohen of the *Gazette* to have three years of Dazzle Dan assembled and delivered to us, by offering him an exclusive. Naturally he demanded specifications.

"Nothing much," I told him on the phone. "Only that Nero Wolfe is out of the detective business because Inspector Cramer is taking his license."

"Quite a gag," Lon conceded.

"No gag. Straight."

"You mean it?"

"We're offering it for publication. Exclusive, unless Cramer's office spills it, and I don't think they will."

"The Getz murder?"

"Yes. Only a couple of paragraphs, because details are not yet available, even to you. I'm out on bail."

"I know you are. This is pie. We'll raid the files and get it over there as soon as we can."

He hung up without pressing for details. Of course that meant he would send Dazzle Dan C.O.D., with a reporter. When the reporter arrived a couple of hours later, shortly after Wolfe had come down from the plant rooms at six o'clock, it wasn't just a man with a notebook, it was Lon Cohen himself. He came to the office with me, dumped a big heavy carton on the floor by my desk, removed his coat and dropped it on the carton to show that Dazzle Dan was his property until paid for, and demanded, "I want the works. What Wolfe said and what Cramer said. A picture of Wolfe studying Dazzle Dan—"

I pushed him into a chair, courteously, and gave him all we were ready to turn loose. Naturally that wasn't enough; it never is. I let him fire questions up to a dozen or so, even answering one or two, and then made it clear that was all for now and I had work to do. He admitted it was a bargain, stuck his notebook in his pocket, and got up and picked up his coat.

"If you're not in a hurry, Mr. Cohen," muttered Wolfe, who had left the interview to me.

Lon dropped the coat and sat down. "I have nineteen years, Mr. Wolfe. Before I retire."

"I won't detain you that long." Wolfe sighed. "I am no longer a detective, but I am a primate and therefore curious. The function of a newspaperman is to satisfy curiosity. Who killed Mr. Getz?"

Lon's brows went up. "Archie Goodwin? It was his gun."

"Nonsense. I'm quite serious. Also I'm discreet. I am excluded from the customary sources of information by the jackassery of Mr. Cramer. I—"

"May I print that?"

"No. None of this. Nor shall I quote you. This is a private conversation. I would like to know what your colleagues are saying but not printing. Who killed Mr. Getz? Miss Lowell? If so, why?"

Lon pulled his lower lip down and let it up again. "You mean we're just talking."

"Yes."

"This might possibly lead to another talk that could be printed."

"It might. I make no commitment." Wolfe wasn't eager.

"You wouldn't. As for Miss Lowell, she has not been scratched. It is said that Getz learned she was chiseling on royalties from makers of Dazzle Dan products and intended to hang it on her. That could have been big money."

"Any names or dates?"

"None that are repeatable. By me. Yet."

"Any evidence?"

"I haven't seen any."

Wolfe grunted. "Mr. Hildebrand. If so, why?"

"That's shorter and sadder. He has told friends about it. He has been with Koven for eight years and was told last week he could leave at the end of the month, and he blamed it on Getz. He might or might not get another job at his age."

Wolfe nodded. "Mr. Jordan?"

Lon hesitated. "This I don't like, but others are talking, so why not us? They say Jordan has painted some pictures, modern stuff, and twice he has tried to get a gallery to show them, two different galleries, and both times Getz has somehow kiboshed it. This has names and dates, but whether because Getz was born a louse or whether he wanted to keep Jordan—"

"I'll do my own speculating. Mr. Getz may not have liked the pictures. Mr. Koven?"

Lon turned a hand over. "Well? What better could you ask? Getz had him buffaloed, no doubt about it. Getz ruled the roost, plenty of evidence on that, and nobody knows why, so the only question is what he had on Koven. It must have been good, but what was it? You say this is a private conversation?"

"Yes."

"Then here's something we got started on just this afternoon. It has to be checked before we print it. That house on Seventy-sixth Street is in Getz's name."

"Indeed." Wolfe shut his eyes and opened them again. "And Mrs. Koven?"

Lon turned his other hand over. "Husband and wife are one, aren't they?"

"Yes. Man and wife make one fool."

Lon's chin jerked up. "I want to print that. Why not?"

"It was printed more than three hundred years ago. Ben Jonson wrote it." Wolfe sighed. "Confound it, what can I do with only a few scraps?" He pointed at the carton. "You want that stuff back, I suppose?"

Lon said he did. He also said he would be glad to go on with the private conversation in the interest of justice and the public welfare, but apparently Wolfe had all the scraps he could use at the moment. After ushering Lon to the door

I went up to my room to spend an hour attending to purely personal matters, a detail that had been too long postponed. I was out of the shower, selecting a shirt, when a call came from Saul Panzer in response to the message I had left. I gave him all the features of the picture that would help and told him to report to Parker's law office in the morning.

After dinner that evening we were all hard at it in the office. Fritz and Theodore were unfolding *Gazette*s, finding the right page and tearing it out. I was banging away at my machine, three pages an hour. Wolfe was at his desk, concentrating on a methodical and exhaustive study of three years of Dazzle Dan. It was well after midnight when he pushed back his chair, arose, stretched, rubbed his eyes, and told us, "It's bedtime. This morass of fatuity has given me indigestion. Good night."

Wednesday morning he tried to put one over. His routine was breakfast in his room, with the morning paper, at eight; then shaving and dressing; then, from nine to eleven, his morning shift up in the plant rooms. He never went to the office before eleven, and the detective business was never allowed to mingle with the orchids. But that Wednesday he fudged. While I was in the kitchen with Fritz, enjoying griddle cakes, Darst's sausage, honey, and plenty of coffee, and going through the morning papers, with two readings of the *Gazette*'s account of Wolfe's enforced retirement, Wolfe sneaked downstairs into the office and made off with a stack of Dazzle Dan.

The way I knew, before breakfast I'd gone in there to straighten up a little, and I am trained to observe. Returning after breakfast, and glancing around before starting at my typewriter, I saw that half of a pile of Dan was gone. I don't think I had ever seen him quite so hot under the collar. I admit I fully approved. Not only did I not make an excuse for a trip up to the roof to catch him at it, but I even took the trouble to be out of the office when he came down at eleven o'clock, to give him a chance to get Dan back unseen.

My first job after breakfast had been to carry out some instructions Wolfe had given me the evening before. Manhattan office hours being what they are, I got no answer at the number of Levay Recorders, Inc., until 9:35. Then it took some talking to get a promise of immediate action, and if it hadn't been for the name of Nero Wolfe I wouldn't have made it. But I got both the promise and the action. A little after ten, two men arrived with cartons of equipment and tool kits, and in less than an hour they were through and gone, and it was a neat and nifty job. It would have taken an expert search to reveal anything suspicious in the office, and the wire to the kitchen, running around the baseboard and on through, wouldn't be suspicious even if seen.

It was hard going at the typewriter on account of the phone ringing, chiefly reporters wanting to talk to Wolfe, and finally I had to ask Fritz in to answer the damn thing and give everybody a brushoff. A call he switched to me was one from the D.A.'s office. They had the nerve to ask me to come down there so they could ask me something. I told them I was busy answering Help Wanted ads and couldn't spare the time.

Half an hour later Fritz switched another one to me. It was Sergeant Purley Stebbins. He was good and sore, beefing about Wolfe having no authority to break the news about losing his license, and it wasn't official yet, and where did I think it would get me refusing to cooperate with the D.A. on a murder when I had discovered the body, and I could have my choice of coming down quick or having a P.D. car come and get me. I let him use up his breath.

"Listen, brother," I told him, "I hadn't heard that the name of this city has been changed to Moscow. If Mr. Wolfe wants to publish it that he's out of business, hoping that someone will pass the hat or offer him a job as doorman, that's his affair. As for my cooperating, nuts. You have already got me sewed up on two charges, and on advice of counsel and my doctor I am staying home, taking aspirin and gargling with prune juice and gin. If you come here, you won't get in without a search warrant. If you come with another warrant for me, say for cruelty to animals because I opened the window, you can either wait on the stoop until I emerge or shoot the door down, whichever you prefer. I am now hanging up."

"If you'll listen a minute—"

"Goodbye, you doublebreasted nitwit."

I cradled the phone, sat thirty seconds to calm down, and resumed at the typewriter. The next interruption came not from the outside but from Wolfe, a little before noon. He was back at his desk, analyzing Dazzle Dan. Suddenly he pronounced my name, and I swiveled.

"Yes, sir."

"Look at this."

He slid a sheet of the *Gazette* across his desk, and I got up and took it. It was a Sunday half page, in color, from four months back. In the first frame Dazzle Dan was scooting along a country road on a motorcycle, passing a roadside sign that read:

PEACHES RIGHT FROM THE TREE!
AGGIE GHOOL AND HAGGIE KROOL

In frame two D.D. had stopped his bike alongside a peach tree full of red and yellow fruit. Standing there were two females, presumably Aggie Ghool and Haggie Krool. One was old and bent, dressed in burlap as near as I could tell; the other was young and pink-cheeked, wearing a mink coat. If you say surely not a mink coat, I say I'm telling what I saw. D.D. was saying, in his balloon, "Gimme a dozen."

Frame three: the young female was handing D.D. the peaches, and the old one was extending her hand for payment. Frame four: the old one was giving D.D. his change from a bill. Frame five: the old one was handing the young one a coin and saying, "Here's your ten per cent, Haggie," and the young one was saying, "Thank you very much, Aggie." Frame six: D.D. was asking Aggie, "Why don't you split it even?" and Aggie was telling him, "Because it's my tree." Frame seven: DD. was off again on the bike, but I felt I had had enough and looked at Wolfe inquiringly.

"Am I supposed to comment?"

"If it would help, yes."

"I pass. If it's a feed from the National Industrialists'

League it's the wrong angle. If you mean the mink coat, Pat Lowell's may not be paid for."

He grunted. "There have been two similar episodes, one each year, with the same characters."

"Then it may be paid for."

"Is that all?"

"It's all for now. I'm not a brain, I'm a typist. I've got to finish this damn report."

I tossed the art back to him and returned to work.

At 12:28 I handed him the finished report, and he dropped D.D. and started on it. I went to the kitchen to tell Fritz I would take on the phone again, and as I re-entered the office it was ringing. I crossed to my desk and got it. My daytime formula was, "Nero Wolfe's office, Archie Goodwin speaking," but with our license gone it was presumably illegal to have an office, so I said, "Nero Wolfe's residence, Archie Goodwin speaking," and heard Saul Panzer's husky voice.

"Reporting in, Archie. No trouble at all. Koven is served. Put it in his hand five minutes ago."

"In the house?"

"Yes. I'll call Parker—"

"How did you get in?"

"Oh, simple. The man that delivers stuff from the Furnari's you told me about has got the itch bad, and it only took ten bucks. Of course after I got inside I had to use my head and legs both, but with your sketch of the layout it was a cinch."

"For you, yes. Mr. Wolfe says satisfactory, which as you know is as far as he ever goes. I say you show promise. You'll call Parker?"

"Yes. I have to go there to sign a paper."

"Okay. Be seeing you."

I hung up and told Wolfe. He lifted his eyes, said, "Ah!" and returned to his report.

After lunch there was an important chore, involving Wolfe, me, our memory of the talk Saturday evening with Koven, and the equipment that had been installed by Levay Recorders, Inc. We spent nearly an hour at it, with three separate tries, before we got it done to Wolfe's satisfaction.

After that it dragged along. The phone calls had fallen off. Wolfe, at his desk, finished with the report, put it in a drawer, leaned back, and closed his eyes. I would just as soon have opened a conversation, but pretty soon his lips started working—pushing out, drawing back and pushing out again—and I knew his brain was busy, so I went to the cabinet for a batch of the germination records and settled down to making entries. He didn't need a license to grow orchids, though the question would soon arise of how to pay the bills.

At four o'clock he left to go up to the plant rooms, and I went on with the records. During the next two hours there were a few phone calls, but none from Koven or his lawyer or Parker. At two minutes past six I was telling myself that Koven was probably drinking himself up to something when two things happened at once: the sound came from the hall of Wolfe's elevator jerking to a stop, and the door-bell rang.

I went to the hall, switched on the stoop light, and took a look through the panel of one-way glass in the front door. It was a mink coat all right, but the hat was different. I marched to the office door and announced, "Miss Patricia Lowell. Will she do?"

He made a face. He seldom welcomes a man crossing his threshold; he never welcomes a woman. "Let her in," he muttered.

I stepped to the front, slid the bolt off, and opened up. "This is the kind of surprise I like," I said heartily. She entered, and I shut the door and bolted it. "Couldn't you find a coconut?"

"I want to see Nero Wolfe," she said in a voice so hard that it was out of character, considering her pink cheeks.

"Sure. This way." I ushered her down the hall and on in. Once in a while Wolfe rises when a woman enters his office, but this time he kept not only his chair but also his tongue. He inclined his head a quarter of an inch when I pronounced her name, but said nothing. I gave her the red leather chair, helped her throw her coat back, and went to my desk.

"So you're Nero Wolfe."

That called for no comment and got none.

"I'm scared to death," she said.

"You don't look it," Wolfe growled.

"I hope I don't; I'm trying not to." She started to put her bag on the little table at her elbow, changed her mind, and kept it in her lap. She took off a glove. "I was sent here by Mr. Koven."

No comment. We were looking at her. She looked at me, then back at Wolfe, and protested, "My God, don't you ever say anything?"

"Only on occasion." Wolfe leaned back. "Give me one."

She compressed her lips. "Mr. Koven sent me," she said, "about the ridiculous suit for damages you have brought. He intends to enter a counterclaim for damage to his reputation through actions of your acknowledged agent, Archie Goodwin. Of course he denies that there is any basis for your suit."

She stopped. Wolfe met her gaze and kept his trap shut.

"That's the situation," she said belligerently.

"Thank you for coming to tell me," Wolfe murmured. "If you'll show Miss Lowell the way out, please, Archie?"

I stood up. She looked at me as if I had offered her a deadly insult, and looked back at Wolfe. "I don't think," she said, "that your attitude is very sensible. I think you and Mr. Koven should come to an agreement on this. Why wouldn't this be the way to do it—say the claims cancel each other, and you abandon yours and he abandons his?"

"Because," Wolfe said dryly, "my claim is valid and his isn't. If you're a member of the bar, Miss Lowell, you should know that this is a little improper, or anyway unconventional. You should be talking with my attorney, not with me."

"I'm not a lawyer, Mr. Wolfe. I'm Mr. Koven's agent and business manager. He thinks lawyers would just make this more of a mess than it is, and I agree with him. He thinks you and he should settle it between you. Isn't that possible?"

"I don't know. We can try. There's a phone. Get him down here."

She shook her head. "He's too upset. I'm sure you'll find it more practical to deal with me, and if we come to an understanding he'll approve, I guarantee that. Why don't we go into it—the two claims?"

"I doubt if it will get us anywhere. For one thing, a factor in both claims is the question who killed Adrian Getz, and why? If it was Mr. Goodwin, Mr. Koven's claim has a footing, and I freely concede it; if it was someone else I concede nothing. If I discussed it with you I would have to begin by considering that aspect; I would have to ask you some pointed questions; and I doubt if you would dare to risk answering them."

"I can always button up. What kind of questions?"

"Well—" Wolfe pursed his lips. "For example, how's the monkey?"

"I can risk answering that. It's sick. It's at the Speyer Hospital. They don't expect it to live."

"Exposure from the open window?"

"Yes. They're very delicate, that kind."

Wolfe nodded. "That table over there by the globe—that pile of stuff on it is Dazzle Dan for the past three years. I've been looking through it. Last August and September a monkey had a prominent role. It was drawn by two different persons, or at least with two different conceptions. In its first seventeen appearances it was depicted maliciously—on a conjecture, by someone with a distaste for monkeys. Thereafter it was drawn sympathetically and humorously. The change was abrupt and noticeable. Why? On instructions from Mr. Koven?"

Pat Lowell was frowning. Her lips parted and went together again.

"You have four choices," Wolfe said bluntly. "The truth, a lie, evasion, or refusal to answer. Either of the last two would make me curious, and I would get my curiosity satisfied somehow. If you try a lie it may work, but I'm an expert on lies and liars."

"There's nothing to lie about. I was thinking back. Mr. Getz objected to the way the monkey was drawn, and Mr. Koven had Mr. Jordan do it instead of Mr. Hildebrand."

"Mr. Jordan likes monkeys?"

"He likes animals. He said the monkey looked like Napoleon."

"Mr. Hildebrand does not like monkeys?"

"He didn't like that one. Rookaloo knew it, of course, and bit him once. Isn't this pretty silly, Mr. Wolfe? Are you going on with this?"

"Unless you walk out, yes. I'm investigating Mr. Koven's counterclaim, and this is how I do it. With any question you have your four choices—and a fifth, too, of course; get up and go. How did you feel about the monkey?"

"I thought it was an awful nuisance, but it had its points as a diversion. It was my fault it was there, since I gave it to Mr. Getz."

"Indeed. When?"

"About a year ago. A friend returning from South America gave it to me, and I couldn't take care of it, so I gave it to him."

"Mr. Getz lived at the Koven house?"

"Yes."

"Then actually you were dumping it onto Mrs. Koven. Did she appreciate it?"

"She has never said so. I didn't—I know I should have considered that. I apologized to her, and she was nice about it."

"Did Mr. Koven like the monkey?"

"He liked to tease it. But he didn't dislike it; he teased it just to annoy Mr. Getz."

Wolfe leaned back and clasped his hands behind his head. "You know, Miss Lowell, I did not find the Dazzle Dan saga hopelessly inane. There is a sustained sardonic tone, some fertility of invention, and even an occasional touch of imagination. Monday evening, while Mr. Goodwin was in jail, I telephoned a couple of people who are supposed to know things and was referred by them to others. I was told that it is generally believed, though not published, that the conception of Dazzle Dan was originally supplied to Mr. Koven by Mr. Getz, that Mr. Getz was the continuing source of inspiration for the story and pictures, and that without him Mr. Koven will be up a stump. What about it?"

Pat Lowell had stiffened. "Talk." She was scornful. "Just cheap talk."

"You should know." Wolfe sounded relieved. "If that belief could be validated I admit I would be up a stump myself. To support my claim against Mr. Koven, and to discredit his against me, I need to demonstrate that Mr. Goodwin did not kill Mr. Getz, either accidentally or otherwise. If he didn't, then who did? One of you five. But all of you had a direct personal interest in the continued success of Dazzle Dan, sharing as you did in the prodigious proceeds; and if Mr. Getz was responsible for the success, why kill him?" Wolfe chuckled. "So you see I'm not silly at all. We've been at it only twenty minutes, and already you've helped me enormously. Give us another four or five hours, and we'll see. By the way."

He leaned forward to press a button at the edge of his desk, and in a moment Fritz appeared.

"There'll be a guest for dinner, Fritz."

"Yes, sir." Fritz went.

"Four or five hours?" Pat Lowell demanded.

"At least that. With a recess for dinner; I banish business from the table. Half for me and half for you. This affair is extremely complicated, and if you came here to get an agreement we'll have to cover it all. Let's see, where were we?"

She regarded him. "About Getz, I didn't say he had nothing to do with the success of Dazzle Dan. After all, so do I. I didn't say he won't be a loss. Everyone knows he was Mr. Koven's oldest and closest friend. We were all quite aware that Mr. Koven relied on him—"

Wolfe showed her a palm. "Please, Miss Lowell, don't spoil it for me. Don't give me a point and then try to snatch it back. Next you'll be saying that Koven called Getz 'the Squirt' to show his affection, as a man will call his dearest friend an old bastard, whereas I prefer to regard it as an inferiority complex, deeply resentful, showing its biceps. Or telling me that all of you, without exception, were inordinately fond of Mr. Getz and submissively grateful to him. Don't forget that Mr. Goodwin spent hours in that house among you and has fully reported to me; also you should know that I had a talk with Inspector Cramer on Monday evening and learned from him some of the plain facts, such as the pillow lying on the floor, scorched and pierced, showing that it had been used to muffle the sound of the shot, and the failure of all of you to prove lack of opportunity."

Wolfe kept going. "But if you insist on minimizing Koven's dependence as a fact, let me assume it as a hypothesis in order to put a question. Say that Koven felt strongly about his debt to Getz and his reliance on him, that he proposed to do something about it, and that he found it necessary to confide in one of you people, to get help or advice. Which of you would he have come to? We must of course put his wife first, ex officio and to sustain convention—and anyway, out of courtesy I must suppose you incapable of revealing your employer's conjugal privities. Which of you three would he have come to—Mr. Hildebrand, Mr. Jordan, or you?"

Miss Lowell was wary. "On your hypothesis, you mean."

"Yes."

"None of us."

"But if he felt he had to?"

"Not with anything as intimate as that. He wouldn't have let himself have to. None of us three has ever got within miles of him on anything really personal."

"Surely he confides in you, his agent and manager?"

"On business matters, yes. Not on personal things."

"Why were all of you so concerned about the gun in his desk?"

"We weren't concerned, not *really* concerned—at least I wasn't. I just didn't like its being there, loaded, so easy to get at, and I knew he didn't have a license for it."

Wolfe kept on about the gun for a good ten minutes—how often had she seen it, had she ever picked it up, and so forth, with special emphasis on Sunday morning, when she and Hildebrand had opened the drawer and looked at it. On that detail she corroborated Hildebrand as I had heard him tell it to Cramer. Finally she balked. She said they weren't getting anywhere, and she certainly wasn't going to stay for dinner if afterward it was only going to be more of the same.

Wolfe nodded in agreement. "You're quite right," he told her. "We've gone as far as we can, you and I. We need all of them. It's time for you to call Mr. Koven and tell him so. Tell him to be here at eight thirty with Mrs. Koven, Mr. Jordan, and Mr. Hildebrand."

She was staring at him. "Are you trying to be funny?" she demanded.

He skipped it. "I don't know," he said, "whether you can handle it properly; if not, I'll talk to him. The validity of my claim, and of his, depends primarily on who killed Mr. Getz. I now know who killed him. I'll have to sell the police but first I want to settle the matter of my claim with Mr. Koven. Tell him that. Tell him that if I have to inform the police before I have a talk with him and the others there will be no compromise on my claim, and I'll collect it."

"This is a bluff."

"Then call it."

"I'm going to." She left the chair and got the coat around her. Her eyes blazed at him. "I'm not such a sap!" She started for the door.

"Get Inspector Cramer, Archie!" Wolfe snapped. He called, "They'll be there by the time you are!"

I lifted the phone and dialed. She was out in the hall, but I heard neither footsteps nor the door opening.

"Hello," I told the transmitter, loud enough. "Manhattan Homicide West? Inspector Cramer, please. This is—"

A hand darted past me, and a finger pressed the button down, and a mink coat dropped to the floor. "Damn you!" she said, hard and cold, but the hand was shaking so that the finger slipped off the button. I cradled the phone.

"Get Mr. Koven's number for her, Archie," Wolfe purred.

At twenty minutes to nine Wolfe's eyes moved slowly from left to right, to take in the faces of our assembled visitors. He was in a nasty humor. He hated to work right after dinner, and from the way he kept his chin down and a slight twitch of a muscle in his cheek I knew it was going to be real work. Whether he had got them there with a bluff or not, it would take more than a bluff to rake in the pot he was after now.

Pat Lowell had not dined with us. Not only had she declined to come along to the dining room, she had also left untouched the tray which Fritz had taken to her in the office. Of course that got Wolfe's goat and probably got some pointed remarks from him, but I wasn't there to hear him because I had gone to the kitchen to check with Fritz on the operation of the installation made by Levay Recorders, Inc. That was the one part of the program that I clearly understood. I was still in the kitchen, rehearsing with Fritz, when the doorbell rang and I went to the front and found them there in a body. They got better hall service than I had got at their place, and also better chair service in the office.

When they were seated Wolfe took them in from left to right—Harry Koven in the red leather chair, then his wife, then Pat Lowell, and, after a gap, Pete Jordan and Byram Hildebrand over toward me. I don't know what impression Wolfe got from his survey, but from where I sat it looked as if he was up against a united front.

"This time," Koven blurted, "you can't cook up a fancy lie with Goodwin. There are witnesses."

He was keyed up. I would have said he had had six drinks, maybe more.

"We won't get anywhere that way, Mr. Koven," Wolfe objected. "We're all tangled up, and it will take more than blather to get us loose. You don't want to pay me a million dollars. I don't want to lose my license. The police don't want to add another unsolved murder to the long list. The central and dominant factor is the violent death of Mr. Getz, and I propose to deal with that if we can get settled—"

"You told Miss Lowell you know who killed him. If so, why don't you tell the police?"

Wolfe's eyes narrowed. "You don't mean that, Mr. Koven—"

"You're damn right I mean it!"

"Then there's a misunderstanding. I heard Miss Lowell's talk with you on the phone, both ends of it. I got the impression that my threat to inform the police about Mr.

56

Getz's death was what brought you here. Now you seem—"

"It wasn't any threat that brought me here! It's that blackmailing suit you started! I want to make you eat it and I'm going to!"

"Indeed. Then I gather that you don't care who gets my information first, you or the police. But I do. For one thing, when I talk to the police I like to be able—"

The doorbell rang. When visitors were present Fritz usually answered the door, but he had orders to stick to his post in the kitchen, so I got up and went to the hall and switched on the stoop light for a look through the one-way glass. One glance was enough. Stepping back into the office, I stood until Wolfe caught my eye.

"The man about the chair," I told him.

He frowned. "Tell him I'm—" He stopped, and the frown cleared. "No. I'll see him. If you'll excuse me a moment?" He pushed his chair back, made it to his feet, and detoured around Koven. I let him precede me into the hall and closed that door before joining him. He strode to the front, peered through the glass, and opened the door. The chain bolt stopped it at a crack of two inches.

Wolfe spoke through the crack. "Well, sir?"

Inspector Cramer's voice was anything but friendly. "I'm coming in."

"I doubt it. What for?"

"Patricia Lowell entered here at six o'clock and is still here. The other four entered fifteen minutes ago. I told you Monday evening to lay off. I told you your license was suspended, and here you are with your office full. I'm coming in."

"I still doubt it. I have no client. My job for Mr. Koven, which you know about, has been finished, and I have sent him a bill. These people are here to discuss an action for damages which I have brought against Mr. Koven. I don't need a license for that. I'm shutting the door."

He tried to, but it didn't budge. I could see the tip of Cramer's toe at the bottom of the crack.

"By God, this does it," Cramer said savagely. "You're through."

"I thought I was already through. But this—"

"I can't hear you! The wind."

"This is preposterous, talking through a crack. Descend to the sidewalk, and I'll come out. Did you hear that?"

"Yes."

"Very well. To the sidewalk."

Wolfe marched to the big old walnut rack and reached for his overcoat. After I had held it for him and handed him his hat, I got my coat and slipped into it and then took a look through the glass. The stoop was empty. A burly figure was at the bottom of the steps. I unbolted the door and opened it, followed Wolfe over the sill, pulled the door shut, and made sure it was locked. A gust of wind pounced on us, slashing at us with sleet. I wanted to take Wolfe's elbow as we went down the steps, thinking where it would leave me if he fell and cracked his skull, but knew I hadn't better.

He made it safely, got his back to the sleety wind, which meant that Cramer had to face it, and raised his voice. "I don't like fighting a blizzard, so let's get to the point. You don't want these people talking with me, but there's nothing you can do about it. You have blundered and you know it. You arrested Mr. Goodwin on a trumpery charge. You came and blustered me and went too far. Now you're afraid I'm going to explode Mr. Koven's lies. More, you're afraid I'm going to catch a murderer and toss him to the District Attorney. So you—"

"I'm not afraid of a damn thing." Cramer was squinting to protect his eyes from the cutting sleet. "I told you to lay off, and by God you're going to. Your suit against Koven is a phony."

"It isn't, but let's stick to the point. I'm uncomfortable. I am not an outdoors man. You want to enter my house. You may, under a condition. The five callers are in my office. There is a hole in the wall, concealed from view in the office by what is apparently a picture. Standing, or on a stool, in a nook at the end of the hall, you can see and hear us in the office. The condition is that you enter quietly— confound it!"

The wind had taken his hat. I made a quick dive and stab but missed, and away it went. He had only had it fourteen years.

"The condition," he repeated, "is that you enter quietly, take your post in the nook, oversee us from there, and give me half an hour. Thereafter you will be free to join us if you think you should. I warn you not to be impetuous. Up to a certain point your presence would make it harder for me, if not impossible, and I doubt if you'll know when that point is reached. I'm after a murderer, and there's one chance in five, I should say, that I'll get him. I want—"

"I thought you said you were discussing an action for damages."

"We are. I'll get either the murderer or the damages. Do you want to harp on that?"

"No."

"You've cooled off, and no wonder, in this hurricane. My hair will go next. I'm going in. If you come along it must be under the condition as stated. Are you coming?"

"Yes."

Wolfe headed for the steps. I passed him to go ahead and unlock the door. When they were inside I closed it and put the bolt back on. They hung up their coats, and Wolfe took Cramer down the hall and around the corner to the nook. I brought a stool from the kitchen, but Cramer shook his head. Wolfe slid the panel aside, making no sound, looked through, and nodded to Cramer. Cramer took a look and nodded back, and we left him. At the door to the office Wolfe muttered about his hair, and I let him use my pocket comb.

From the way they looked at us as we entered you might have thought they suspected we had been in the cellar fusing a bomb, but one more suspicion wouldn't make it any harder. I circled to my desk and sat. Wolfe got himself back in place, and passed his eyes over them.

"I'm sorry," he said politely, "but that was unavoidable. Suppose we start over"—he looked at Koven—"say, with your surmise to the police that Getz was shot by Mr. Goodwin accidentally in a scuffle. That's absurd. Getz was shot with a cartridge that had been taken from your gun and put into Goodwin's gun. Manifestly Goodwin couldn't have done that, since when he first saw your gun Getz was already dead. Therefore—"

"That's not true!" Koven cut in. "He had seen it before, when he came to my office. He could have gone back later and got the cartridges."

Wolfe glared at him in astonishment. "Do you really dare, sir, in front of me, to my face, to cling to that fantastic tale you told the police? That rigmarole?"

"You're damn right I do!"

"Pfui." Wolfe was disgusted. "I had hoped, here together, we were prepared to get down to reality. It would have been better to adopt your suggestion to take my information to the police. Perhaps—"

"I made no such suggestion!"

"In this room, Mr. Koven, some fifteen minutes ago?"

"No!"

Wolfe made a face. "I see," he said quietly. "It's impossible to get on solid ground with a man like you, but I still have to try. Archie, bring the tape from the kitchen, please?"

I went. I didn't like it. I thought he was rushing in. Granting that he had been jostled off his stride by Cramer's arrival, I felt that it was far from one of his best performances, and this looked like a situation where nothing less than his best would do. So I went to the kitchen, passing Cramer in his nook without a glance, told Fritz to stop the machine and wind, and stood and scowled at it turning. When it stopped I removed the wheel and slipped it into a carton and, carton in hand, returned to the office.

"We're waiting," Wolfe said curtly.

That hurried me. There was a stack of similar cartons on my desk, and in my haste I knocked them over as I was putting down the one I had brought. It was embarrassing with all eyes on me, and I gave them a cold look as I crossed to the cabinet to get the player. It needed a whole corner of my desk, and I had to shove the tumbled cartons aside to make room. Finally, I had the player in position and connected, and the wheel of tape, taken from the carton, in place.

"All right?" I asked Wolfe.

"Go ahead."

I flipped the switch. There was a crackle and a little spitting, and then Wolfe's voice came:

"It's not that, Mr. Koven, not at all. I doubt if it's worth it to you, considering the size of my minimum fee, to hire me for anything so trivial as finding a stolen gun, or even discovering the thief. I should think—"

"No!" Wolfe bellowed.

I switched it off. I was flustered. "Excuse it," I said. "The wrong tape."

"Must I do it myself?" Wolfe asked sarcastically.

I muttered something, turning the wheel to rewind. I removed it, pawed among the cartons, picked one, took out the wheel, put it on, and turned the switch. This time the voice that came on was not Wolfe's but Koven's—loud and clear.

"This time you can't cook up a fancy lie with Goodwin. There are witnesses."

Then Wolfe: *"We won't get anywhere that way, Mr. Koven. We're all tangled up, and it will take more than blather to get us loose. You don't want to pay me a million dollars. I don't want to lose my license. The police don't want to add another unsolved murder to the long list. The central and dominant factor is the violent death of Mr. Getz, and I propose to deal with that if we can get settled—"*

Koven: *"You told Miss Lowell you know who killed him. If so, why don't you tell the police?"*

Wolfe: *"You don't mean that, Mr. Koven—"*

Koven: *"You're damn right I mean it!"*

Wolfe: *"Then there's a misunderstanding. I heard Miss Lowell's talk with you on the phone, both ends of it. I got the impression that my threat to inform the police—"*

"That's enough!" Wolfe called. I turned it off. Wolfe looked at Koven. "I would call that," he said dryly, "a suggestion that I take my information to the police. Wouldn't you?"

Koven wasn't saying. Wolfe's eyes moved. "Wouldn't you, Miss Lowell?"

She shook her head. "I'm not an expert on suggestions."

Wolfe left her. "We won't quarrel over terms, Mr. Koven. You heard it. Incidentally, about the other tape you heard the start of through Mr. Goodwin's clumsiness, you may wonder why I haven't given it to the police to refute you. Monday evening, when Inspector Cramer came to see me, I still considered you as my client and I didn't want to discomfit you until I heard what you had to say. Before Mr. Cramer left he had made himself so offensive that I was disinclined to tell him anything whatever. Now you are no longer my client. We'll discuss this matter realistically or not at all. I don't care to badger you into an explicit statement that you lied to the police; I'll leave that to you and them; I merely insist that we proceed on the basis of what we both know to be the truth. With that understood—"

"Wait a minute," Pat Lowell put in. "The gun was in the drawer Sunday morning. I saw it."

"I know you did. That's one of the knots in the tangle, and we'll come to it." His eyes swept the arc. "We want to know who killed Adrian Getz. Let's get at it. What do we know about him or her? We know a lot.

"First, he took Koven's gun from the drawer sometime previous to last Friday and kept it somewhere. For that gun was put back in the drawer when Goodwin's was removed shortly before Getz was killed, and cartridges from it were placed in Goodwin's gun.

"Second, the thought of Getz continuing to live was for some reason so repugnant to the murderer as to be intolerable.

"Third, he knew the purpose of Koven's visit here Saturday evening, and of Goodwin's errand at the Koven house on Monday, and he knew the details of the procedure planned by Koven and Goodwin. Only with—"

"I don't know them even yet," Hildebrand squeaked.

"Neither do I," Pete Jordan declared.

"The innocent can afford ignorance," Wolfe told them. "Enjoy it if you have it. Only with that knowledge could he have devised his intricate scheme and carried it out.

"Fourth, his mental processes are devious but defective. His deliberate and spectacular plan to make it appear that Goodwin had killed Getz, while ingenious in some respects, was in others witless. Going to Koven's office to get Goodwin's gun from the drawer and placing Koven's gun there, transferring the cartridges from Koven's gun to Goodwin's, proceeding to the room below to find Getz asleep, shooting him in the head, using a pillow to muffle the sound—all that was well enough, competently conceived and executed, but then what? Wanting to make sure that the gun would be quickly found on the spot, a quite unnecessary precaution, he slipped it into the monkey's cage. That was probably improvisation and utterly brainless. Mr. Goodwin couldn't possibly be such a vapid fool.

"Fifth, he hated the monkey deeply and bitterly, either on its own account or because of its association with Getz. Having just killed a man, and needing to leave the spot with all possible speed, he went and opened a window, from only one conceivable motive. That took a peculiar, unexampled malevolence. I admit it was effective. Miss Lowell tells me the monkey is dying.

"Sixth, he placed Koven's gun in the drawer Sunday morning and, after it had been seen there, took it out again. That was the most remarkable stratagem of all. Since there was no point in putting it there unless it was to be seen, he arranged that it should be seen. Why? It could only have been that he already knew what was to happen on Monday when Mr. Goodwin came, he had already conceived his scheme for framing Goodwin for the homicide, and he thought he was arranging in advance to discredit Goodwin's story. So he not only put the gun in the drawer Sunday morning, he also made sure its presence would be noted—and not, of course, by Mr. Koven."

Wolfe focused on one of them. "You saw the gun in the drawer Sunday morning, Mr. Hildebrand?"

"Yes." The squeak was off pitch. "But I didn't put it there!"

"I didn't say you did. Your claim to innocence has not yet been challenged. You were in the workroom, went up to consult Mr. Koven, encountered Mrs. Koven one flight up, were told by her that Mr. Koven was still in bed, ascended to the office, found Miss Lowell there, and you pulled the drawer open and both of you saw the gun there. Is that correct?"

"I didn't go up there to look in that drawer. We just—"

"Stop meeting accusations that haven't been made. It's a bad habit. Had you been upstairs earlier that morning?"

"No!"

"Had he, Miss Lowell?"

"Not that I know of." She spoke slowly, with a drag, as if she had only so many words and had to count them. "Our looking into the drawer was only incidental."

"Had he, Mrs. Koven?"

The wife jerked her head up. "Had he what?" she demanded.

"Had Mr. Hildebrand been upstairs earlier that morning?"

She looked bewildered. "Earlier than what?"

"You met him in the second-floor hall and told him that your husband was still in bed and that Miss Lowell was up in the office. Had he been upstairs before that? That morning?"

"I haven't the slightest idea."

"Then you don't say that he had been?"

"I know nothing about it."

"There's nothing as safe as ignorance—or as dangerous." Wolfe spread his gaze again. "To complete the list of what we know about the murderer. Seventh and last, his repugnance to Getz was so extreme that he even scorned the risk that by killing Getz he might be killing Dazzle Dan. How essential Getz was to Dazzle Dan—"

"*I* made Dazzle Dan!" Harry Koven roared. "Dazzle Dan is mine!" He was glaring at everybody. "*I* am Dazzle Dan!"

"For God's sake, shut up, Harry!" Pat Lowell said.

Koven's chin was quivering. He needed three quick drinks.

"I was saying," Wolfe went on, "that I do not know how essential Getz was to Dazzle Dan. The testimony conflicts. In any case the murderer wanted him dead. I've identified the murderer for you by now, surely?"

"You have not," Pat Lowell said aggressively.

"Then I'll specify." Wolfe leaned forward at them. "But first let me say a word for the police, particularly Mr. Cramer. He is quite capable of unraveling a tangle like this, with its superficial complexities. What flummoxed him was Mr. Koven's elaborate lie, apparently corroborated by Miss Lowell and Mr. Hildebrand. If he had had the gumption to proceed on the assumption that Mr. Goodwin and I were telling the truth and all of it, he would have found it simple. This should be a lesson to him."

Wolfe considered a moment. "It might be better to specify by elimination. If you recall my list of seven facts about the murderer, that is child's play. Mr. Jordan, for instance, is eliminated by Number Six; he wasn't there Sunday morning. Mr. Hildebrand is eliminated by three or four of them, especially Number Six again; he had made no earlier trip upstairs. Miss Lowell is eliminated, for me, by Number Four and Five; and I am convinced that none of the three I have named can meet the requirements of Number Three. I do not believe that Mr. Koven would have confided in any of them so intimately—"

"Hold it!" The gruff voice came from the doorway.

Heads jerked around. Cramer advanced and stopped at Koven's left, between him and his wife. There was dead silence. Koven had his neck twisted to stare up at Cramer, then suddenly he fell apart and buried his face in his hands.

Cramer, scowling at Wolfe, boiling with rage, spoke. "Damn you, if you had given it to us! You and your number game!"

"I can't give you what you won't take," Wolfe said bitingly. "You can have her now. Do you want more help? Mr. Koven was still in bed Sunday morning when two of them saw the gun in the drawer. More? Spend the night interrogating Mr. Hildebrand; I'll stake my license against your badge that he'll remember that when he spoke with Mrs. Koven in the hall she said something that caused him to open the drawer and look at the gun. Still more? Take all the contents of her room to your laboratory. She must have hid the gun among her intimate things, and you should find evidence. You can't put him on the stand and ask him if and when he told her what he was doing; he can't testify against his wife; but—"

Mrs. Koven stood up. She was pale but under control, perfectly steady. She looked down at the back of her husband's bent head.

Cramer, in one short step, was at her elbow.

"Harry!" she said, softly insistent. "Take me home."

His head lifted and turned to look at her. I couldn't see his face. "Sit down, Marcy," he said. "I'll handle this." He looked at Wolfe. "If you've got a record of what I said here Saturday, all right. I lied to the cops. So what? I didn't want to—"

"Be quiet, Harry," Pat Lowell blurted at him. "Get a lawyer and let him talk. Don't say anything."

Wolfe nodded. "That's good advice. Especially, Mr. Koven, since I hadn't quite finished. It is a matter of record that Mr. Getz not only owned the house you live in but also that he owned Dazzle Dan and permitted you to take only ten per cent of the proceeds."

Mrs. Koven dropped back into the chair and froze, staring at him. Wolfe spoke to her. "I suppose, madam, that after you killed him you went to his room to look for documents and possibly found some and destroyed them. That must have been part of your plan last week when you first took the gun from the drawer—to destroy all evidence of his ownership of Dazzle Dan after killing him. That was foolish, since a man like Mr. Getz would surely not leave invaluable papers in so accessible a spot, and they will certainly be found; we can leave that to Mr. Cramer. When I said it is a matter of record, I meant a record that I have inspected and have in my possession."

Wolfe pointed. "That stack of stuff on that table is Dazzle Dan for the past three years. In one episode, repeated annually with variations, he buys peaches from two characters named Aggie Ghool and Haggie Krool, and Aggie Ghool saying that she owns the tree, gives Haggie Krool ten per cent of the amount received and pockets the rest. A.G. are the initials of Adrian Getz; H.K. are the initials of Harry Koven. It is not credible that that is coincidence or merely a prank, especially since the episode was repeated annually. Mr. Getz must have had a singularly contorted psyche, taking delight as he did in hiding the fact of his ownership and control of that monster, but compelling the nominal owner to publish it each year in a childish allegory. For a meager ten per cent of the—"

"Not of the net," Koven objected. "Ten per cent of the gross. Over four hundred a week clear, and I—"

He stopped. His wife had said, "You worm." Leaving her chair, she stood looking down at him.

"You worm!" she said in bitter contempt. "Not even a worm. Worms have guts."

She whirled to face Wolfe. "All right, you've got him. The one time he ever acted like a man, and he didn't have the guts to see it through. Getz owned Dazzle Dan, that's right. When he got the idea and sold it, years ago, and took Harry in to draw it and front it, Harry should have insisted on an even split right then and didn't. He never had it in him to insist on anything, and never would, and Getz knew it. When Dazzle Dan caught on, and the years went by and it kept getting bigger and bigger, Getz didn't mind Harry having the name and the fame as long as he owned it and got the money. You said he had a contorted psyche; maybe that was it, only that's not what I'd call it. Getz was a vampire."

"I'll accept that," Wolfe said.

"That's the way it was when I met Harry, but I didn't know it until we were married, two years ago. I admit Getz might not have got killed if it hadn't been for me. When I found out how it was I tried to talk sense into Harry. I told him his name had been connected with Dazzle Dan so long that Getz would have to give him a bigger share, at least half, if he demanded it. He claimed he tried, but he just wasn't man enough. I told him his name was so well known that he could cut loose and start another one on his own, but he wasn't man enough for that, either. He's not a man, he's a worm. I didn't let up. I kept after him, I admit that. I'll admit it on the witness stand if I have to. And I admit I didn't know him as well as I thought I did. I didn't know there was any danger of making him desperate enough to commit murder. I didn't know he had it in him. Of course he'll break down, but if he says I knew that he had decided to kill Getz I'll have to deny it because it's not true. I didn't."

Her husband was staring up at her, his mouth hanging

open.

"I see." Wolfe's voice was hard and cold. "First you plan to put it on a stranger, Mr. Goodwin—indeed, two strangers, for I am in it, too. That failing, you put it on your husband." He shook his head. "No, madam. Your silliest mistake was opening the window to kill the monkey, but there were others. Mr. Cramer?"

Cramer had to take only one step to get her arm.

"Oh, God!" Koven groaned.

Pat Lowell said to Wolfe in a thin sharp voice, "So this is what you worked me for."

She was a tough baby, too, that girl.

by CHARLOTTE ARMSTRONG

THE LIGHT NEXT DOOR

We have linked Charlotte Armstrong's "The Light Next Door" with Patricia Highsmith's "The Empty Birdhouse" in what might be called "A Pair of Strange Stories"—and that they are. Strange, both of them—but utterly different from one another. And yet we have the oddest feeling that in some mysterious and magical way the two authors started with basically the same "germ" of an idea. If that is so—and judge for yourself after you have read the two stories—how interesting that the plots should grow and develop so differently, should evolve into such totally different stories. . .

Having loafed all morning, Howard Lamboy was improving the holiday afternoon, but Miggs, the dog, thought that raking leaves in the back yard was a jolly game, and a part of the fun for him was to scatter all the piles. After much haranguing, and gesturing with the rake, Howard had just conceded that he was never going to get anywhere until Miggs was banished indoors. He had his hand in the dog's collar when the pouched face of his neighbor poked around the back corner of the garage. It was followed by the thin body, which stationed itself on the other side of the knee-high hedge.

"Hi," said Ralph Sidwell, with his usual gloomy diffidence.

"Oh, hi, Ralph," said Howard. "How's every little thing?" Then he bit his tongue, because the man was a bridegroom, and his bride, whatever else, was certainly not little; and while Howard was filled with normal human curiosity he hadn't meant to be crude.

"Fine," said Ralph absently. "Say, by the way, that dog of yours made off with a pillow from my place. Seen any traces?"

"What?" Miggs was writhing, head to tip of tail, like a line of light on choppy water. Howard let him go and the dog gamboled over to the hedge to sniff welcome. The neighbor looked sourly down at the Dalmatian.

"Now, what's all this?" said Howard genially. "What the devil would Miggs want with a pillow? He's got a pillow. No, I haven't seen any traces. What do you mean?"

"Francine," said Ralph coldly, "put a bed pillow out on the back balcony to air and it fell off the railing. Your dog hauled it away."

"I don't believe it," said Howard. "Where is it?"

"That's what I was asking you."

"*Bed* pillow?" Howard was incredulous. "I doubt he'd bury a thing like that, you know."

"Well, it's gone," said Ralph gruffly.

"Well, I'm very sorry," said Howard, "but I don't know a thing about it and neither does my dog."

"How do you know he doesn't?" said Ralph. "My wife saw him."

"She recognized him?" Howard was still.

"Black and white spots," said Ralph in triumph.

"Well, well! Only black and white dog in the world, eh? I can tell you, Miggs didn't bring any bed pillow home, and you tell me where else he would have brought it."

"He did *something* with it," said Ralph stubbornly.

"I don't think so," said Howard. "Excuse us, please?"

He grabbed the dog's collar again and dragged Miggs off to the kitchen door.

"What's the matter?" said Stella.

"Oh, boy!" said Howard eloquently.

After a while he told her.

"Okay," Stella said, "Miggs didn't do it. So it's a mistake. But, Howard, what makes you so mad?"

"Aw, it was his attitude."

"In what way?"

"So damned unreasonable."

"Listen, he's only been married two days," said Stella. "It's whatever her little heart desires, for gosh sakes."

"Fine way she's setting up diplomatic relations."

But Stella said, "A second marriage, at their ages, is probably pretty upsetting. Have a little human understanding."

"Well, it's Miggs *I* understand," said Howard. "I know him better, for one thing."

The fact was, he didn't know Ralph Sidwell at all. Howard was 44 years old and his neighbor must be in his middle fifties. Howard preferred to think of this as a whole other generation. Ralph and his first wife, Milly, had been living next door when the Lamboys moved in eight years ago. While the Sidwells had not called, they had been pleasant enough over-the-fence; but the relationship had never become more than a hot-enough-for-you or sure-need-rain sort of thing.

Milly Sidwell, a personality of no apparent force, had taken a notion to die in the distance, having succumbed, according to the newspaper, while visiting relatives in Ohio. When the widower had returned, without a wife or her body to bury here, the Lamboys had bestirred themselves to make a condolence call. This had evidently either surprised or alarmed the man to the point of striking him dumb. It hadn't been a very satisfactory occasion.

Later Stella had asked him over to dinner, three separate times, which invitations Ralph had refused, as if he couldn't believe his ears, and they must be mad. So the Lamboys had given up. For the last three years Ralph Sidwell had lived alone, next door, taking his meals out somewhere, coming and going with a minimum of contact. The Lamboys, being involved in warm and roaring communication with their neighbors on the other side, didn't miss what they had never had.

Now, suddenly, Ralph had taken unto himself a second wife.

The Lamboys had not been invited to the wedding which, indeed, scarcely seemed to have been a social occasion. Wednesday morning (only yesterday), Ralph had been standing in his own driveway when Howard drove out; Ralph had hailed him, and had announced, rather stiffly, that he had been married on his lunch hour the day before. He wanted the Lamboys to meet the bride.

Howard had shut off his motor and got out of the car in honor of the news. (The least he could do!) Stella had come running out in her morning garb of robe and apron, and

Francine Sidwell—the widow Noble, that was—had come out of her kitchen to be presented.

She had been dressed neatly. (Stella confessed later that she had felt mortified, herself.) But there was no better word for Francine than "fat"—unless it was "enormous."

Stella reported that after Howard had driven off to his office they had told her that they had first met in a laundromat. "She's a marvelous cook," Ralph had said, and that was the end of the conversation.

Although Stella said mischievously that probably Ralph only wanted to make sure they didn't think he was living in sin, she was prepared to accept and adopt a neighborly approach. But it was only right to let them severely alone for "a while"—a period that would correspond to the honeymoon they evidently were not taking.

This was only Thursday. Howard was thinking, with human understanding, that a second "honeymoon" might not be all honey when Miggs, that lovable clown, placed his jaw in warm devotion on Howard's ankle. "That's my fella," said Howard. "Love me, love my dog."

This wasn't what he meant. He didn't expect the Sidwells to *love* him, but they ought to notice what *he* loved.

On Saturday, Howard was out moseying along the line of the scraggly hedge between the lots and wondering what the hedge disliked about its situation, when Ralph Sidwell came out of his own back door, marching, to accost him.

"Now," he said, with no other preliminary, "you are going to have to tie that dog up." He pointed at Miggs, whose name he ought to know perfectly well, with a shaking finger. "We have a right," he sputtered, "to hang anything we like on our own clothesline and have if safe. Your dog—"

"His name," said Howard coolly, "is Miggs."

"Your stupid animal," said Ralph, "has taken my great-grandmother's patchwork quilt! And that's a priceless heirloom! It can't be replaced." He was shouting. "My great-grandmother made it when she was a *girl!*"

"Hold it," said Howard. "Now calm down, will you?"

"By *hand!*" yelled the neighbor.

"Listen, I'm sure she did," said Howard. "But what has that got to do with Miggs? He wouldn't take a quilt off your clothesline."

"If he didn't, who did?"

"How would I know? I suppose your wife saw him again? She must have spots before her eyes."

"Don't you insult my wife!"

"Then quit insulting my dog."

"Where is my great-grandmother's quilt?"

"I haven't the faintest idea and I couldn't care less!"

Miggs, getting into the spirit of things, began to growl. Stella came running out of the house. "What are you bellowing about?"

By now Howard was speechless. Ralph was still pointing at Miggs.

"Oh, honey?" Out of the back door of the other house (identical in floor plan except that right was left) came the bride. Francine was hurrying and her flesh jiggled and bounced. She had in her arms a patchwork quilt, all blues and whites and greens. "Oh, honey," she panted. "Look, I found it. It's all right, I found it."

"Well!" said Ralph hotly. He turned and gave Howard a hard glare. The look said: Don't you dare say I shouldn't have been so mad at you, because I am *still* mad.

Miggs, who understood hostility in every language, even the silent ones, barked, and Francine clutched the quilt and began to walk backward. (Was she afraid?) Howard rose in his wrath and simply strode past the hedge. "Let me see that," he demanded.

Francine screamed lightly.

"Hey, Miggs, whoa!" cried Stella, grabbing the dog's collar and hanging on with all her weight.

Ralph Sidwell said, "Don't touch it. That's *mine*."

"Yours, your great-grandmother," yelled Howard. "You show me my dog's toothmarks or his claw prints or *any* evidence—" He snatched up the quilt by a corner. It was a lovely old thing, on the fragile side. Francine kept backing away, and Howard had to let go to keep from tearing the treasure. "For your information," he howled, "*my* dog doesn't eat tomatoes."

"Okay, I apologize," Ralph screeched, as angrily as he could.

"Oh, honey, I'm sorry," Francine was saying to her bridegroom. (She was afraid!) "Oh, listen, Mrs. Lamboy, I'm so sorry—"

Stella bent her head as if she were the Queen and Francine the commoner. "Come, Miggs. Come, Howard," she said, rounding up her own fierce creatures.

They persuaded Miggs into the house. Howard flung himself down in his den and poured some beer and did it wrong and caused too big a head and swore and blew out his breath in a long "Whew!" The dog lay down at his feet and thumped the floor with his tail, waiting for praise. "That's right, pal," said Howard. "You didn't do it, did you? Darn idiots!"

Stella was cooling off, by herself, in the kitchen, and it didn't take her long. She came in and said. "We're not going to have this, you know."

"Darned right."

"I mean we're not going to have any feud on," she said grimly. "Of all the miserable things in this world a feud with neighbors is the stupidest. And *we* are not going to have one."

"Okay. Let them lay off my dog."

"What's this 'my dog' all the time?" she said. "He's my dog too, and I love him dearly, and I know he's not guilty, as well as you do. But I am not going to get into a silly fight with neighbors. Ralph apologized."

"Yeah, some apology," Howard scoffed. But he saw her point. He wasn't really as childish as this. So it was agreed that Stella would call on her neighbor, as soon as seemed correct, and—well, just do the right thing and *be* neighborly.

So on Monday morning, Howard being at work, Stella made a luscious pie. She phoned Mrs. Sidwell and announced that she would like to come over and call. Would three o'clock be all right? Francine, in a fluster, said it would, of course.

So Stella dressed herself nicely, but not too formally, and went down her own front walk and around on the public sidewalk to the neighbors' walk and up to their front door and rang the bell. She had been in this house only once before. She had no way to assess what changes the new mistress may have made in the decor or the atmosphere. The house was neat to the point of seeming bare. It "felt" like a man's house. But Ralph was not there.

Francine had dressed herself more or less "up" for company. She made exclamations over the high pie, delicate under its burden of whipped cream. She took Stella into the dining room and produced coffee with which she served generous portions of the peace offering. Stella, eating her own pie (and she wished she didn't have to because *she* did count calories), made the normal approaches.

The weather. Bright days. Cool nights. How long the Lamboys had lived here. That they had a daughter away at college. Just the one child. That the houses were small but comfortable, weren't they? A development, yes. You would hardly know any more that they were all alike, what with each owner using paint and trellis, shrub and vine, in an individual way. This had always delighted Stella. But Francine wanted, she said, the recipe.

Oh? Stella recited the recipe for her pie. And how did Mrs. Sidwell like the neighborhood?

Well, Francine thought it was very nice and the house was very nice and the market was very convenient and the pie was *delicious!* Oh, yes, she had been a widow for some years, all alone, yes, and she *was* enjoying this pie. Would Mrs. Lamboy take another piece? No? Then Mrs. Sidwell would.

Stella, smiling and murmuring, watched and listened and thought to herself: No wonder she's so fat! She also was getting a strange impression that the woman beside her was, in truth, a gaunt starving creature, and the flesh in which she was wrapped was a blanket to keep cold bones from shaking apart—an insulation to keep fine drawn nerves from splitting and shattering at the slightest sensation. But everything was going smoothly, on the surface, so Stella brought up the matter of the quilt.

She was so glad it had been neither lost nor damaged.

Francine said, "I washed and ironed it and it's as good as new."

This seemed to Stella to be an odd way to speak of an antique, but she went on to deplore any misunderstanding about the dog. "We know his habits so well, you see. He is really a harmless old fellow. Wonderful with children. Oh, he loves everybody, including burglars, I'm afraid. Of course, maybe you are a cat person? I seem to remember Mrs. Sid — oh, I'm sorry."

Francine was staring at her. Her features were lost in the rounded flesh. It was hard to imagine what kind of nose or chin she had. But her eyes were peering out of their rosy nests, and surely there was fear in them.

"All I meant," said Stella, "some people adore cats and can't stand—" (She hadn't meant to mention the first Mrs. Sidwell—she must be more careful.)

"I don't care for pets, not much," said Francine and stuffed and totally filled her mouth with whipped cream.

After a decently brief interval Stella went home, thoughtful and a little dismayed. She told Howard at dinnertime that there was now peace, and for pity's sake not to break it. Because peace, she went on to confide, was about all there could ever be between Stella Lamboy and the woman next door.

"It's not that I don't *like* her," Stella said. "It's just that I didn't find one thing—there's just no—well, maybe it isn't fair after only fifteen minutes but there wasn't *one* spark! The only thing she seems to care about is food. She didn't want to know what I care about."

"Obviously," said Howard, "she doesn't care about being fashionably slim."

Stella shuddered and wondered why she did. "She admitted she doesn't care much for pets," she said. "But she's not—well, aggressive about it."

"Miggs can coexist," said Howard loftily, "as long as there is no aggression from out across the border."

But he was thinking: Who would spill tomato juice on an antique patchwork quilt? Or was it something else that I saw on it? The color of—blood?

That night Howard got himself trapped in the Late Show. When he took Miggs out on his leash it was after midnight. The street was quiet; the tweedy dark was fresh and cool. As he ambled down the block, with the dog's eager life tugging, kitelike, on the leash in his hand, Howard fell into what he sometimes called, to himself, his "cosmic" thoughts.

Suburban, ordinary, these undistinguished rows of boxes, set among the trees, all silent now. What have we here, he mused. Everything commonplace. You betcha! *Commonplace* stuff—like birth, death, love, hate, fear, hope. In his imagination he could lift the lids from some of these boxes, lift them right off. He knew one box that held patient suffering, another that rang with music all day long. He couldn't help telling himself that every box on the street was a package of human mystery—which was quite commonplace, he thought complacently.

When he turned at the end of the block it was his fancy to cross over and come back on the other side of the street. Suddenly, in the upper story of the house next door to his—the Sidwells'—he seemed to see a wash of light. No room lit up. But something paler than the dark had washed along the windows from the inside. Burglars, he thought at once. There it went again. Howard began to walk on his toes, although now the house remained dark, and Miggs hadn't noticed anything.

Howard crept on until he was directly across from the Sidwell house and there, again, came that washing light, from inside, but now on the ground floor.

He hauled on the leash and struck across to his own house, keeping an uneasy eye to his right. Stella was asleep in her bed, trusting and innocent and *alone*. He must be careful. But his own house seemed to breathe in peace, so he stood quietly on his own porch until Miggs whined a question. Then he unlocked the door and took the dog in.

Miggs curled around on his own cushion in the kitchen and Howard patted the freshened fur, meanwhile peering out the window. There *was* a light of some sort in the kitchen over there, across the two driveways. But there was a shade, or drawn curtains. He couldn't quite see in.

And he could hear nothing.

Nothing was happening. No more mysterious glimmers.

Finally, Howard locked all his doors and went up to bed. But he kept his ear on the night, until he remembered there was a better ear than his, downstairs.

The next morning, as Howard went to get out his car, he heard a futile whirring and whining in the Sidwells' garage. So he leaned over the hedge. "Trouble?"

It seemed that Ralph was going to work (so much for honeymoons!) but his darned battery— He wasn't going to drive Francine's old crate, either. So Howard offered him a lift. They discovered a useful coincidence of routes, Ralph ran into his house to give Francine his Auto Club card, then got in beside Howard, breathless and grateful.

Ralph worked for the Gas Company. He'd get home all right. A fellow worker lived not too far from here.

"Say," said Howard after a while, "anybody prowling around in your house last night?"

"What?"

"Well, I just happened to be walking the dog. Wondered if you had a burglar," Howard went on cheerfully.

"I wake up once or twice," said Ralph, bristling. "I'd know if we had a burglar."

Howard felt sheepish. "Well, I was really wondering if anybody felt sick. You know, had to get up and take medicine or something?"

"Not at all," said Ralph angrily.

Howard was sorry he had said anything. Whatever intimate ceremonies might take place at night in his neighbor's house were *not* his business. He said, "Maybe you ought to keep a dog. I was thinking, last night, he'd hear the softest burglar in the world. Trouble is, you take Miggs, he's all the time hearing things no man can *ever* hear. This can be upsetting, too."

"I am not," said Ralph furiously, "superstitious. And I don't intend to get that way."

Howard judged it best to change the subject.

He said to his wife that evening, "They're bugging me."

"Who are?"

"Next door. I don't know."

"What don't you know?"

"I don't know *anything*." Howard stared at her somewhat hostilely, because he was feeling foolish. "I don't know what he meant by 'superstitious.' And there's something else I can't get out of my head."

"So put it into mine," she invited.

"It bugs me that I saw a red stain of some kind on that quilt."

"*What* kind?" she said.

"Okay," he confessed. "You know the classics. Ever think of this? How do we know what *really* happened to Milly Sidwell?"

When Stella did not laugh it occurred to Howard, with a familiar surprise, that he loved her very much, darned if he didn't. She said in a minute, "I don't see how he could have buried Milly in his back yard without *Miggs* knowing all about it, do you?"

"That's right," said Howard, relaxing.

"Of course, in the cellar—" She raised an eyebrow at him.

"They've got no cellar," said Howard at once. All these little houses sat on concrete slabs. There were no cellars. Howard could think of nowhere to hide a body in *his* house, so he felt cheered.

"Anyhow, that's silly," Stella said indulgently, now that he was cheered. And then she added, "Ralph didn't *care* enough about Milly to murder her." She hoped he wouldn't want her to explain. She wasn't sure she could.

But Howard said, "I'll tell you what, Stell. Why don't we ask them over for a barbecue on Sunday? Out in the back yard? Real informal?"

"Why?" she asked calmly, trusting him to know that she was only wondering, not saying "No."

"Because," he answered, "they bug me."

"Me, too," said Stella in a minute.

Stella extended the invitation over the phone, coaxed a little, saying that it was right next door, just the four of them, no special trouble would be gone to, everything very informal, just wear any old clothes. Howard was very good with steaks on charcoal. Francine said she would ask Ralph.

On Wednesday morning, when Howard appeared, Ralph was backing out his revived vehicle. He stopped. "Say, Howard?"

"Yeah?"

"Listen, Francine would like to come over on Sunday. The only thing—"

"Yeah?"

"I'm wondering, could you lock up your dog?"

"What do you mean, lock him up?"

"Well, Francine, she's nervous about coming over. She's afraid, I guess, of dogs."

"Well," said Howard, "Miggs isn't going to think much of the idea, but sure, he can stay in the house. You come along over, both of you."

So the invitation was accepted.

Sure enough, on Sunday, Miggs saw no reason to conceal his anguish at being incarcerated while something interesting was going on behind the house. Howard and Stella did their best, carrying trays of food out to the redwood table, lighting the candles in their glass globes, offering drinks and tidbits, Howard fussing over his coals.

The guests didn't help. The meal was uncomfortable, speech stiff, dull, pumped up. No spark, as Stella had said before. Ralph was an unresponsive man, Howard decided. That was a good word for him. He seemed to be locked up inside himself. Lonely, you could say. As for Francine, she ate well.

When it was time for dessert, Howard went into the kitchen with a trayload of dirty dishes. Under full instructions he was trusted to return with a trayload of sweets, the ice cream and cake, while Stella poured the coffee and kept the lame talk limping along.

Howard stood over the sink, rinsing off the plates while he was at it, with Miggs coiling and curling around his legs. Begging and apologizing. Whatever I did to offend you, forgive me? Please, I would so like to come to the party?

Howard felt bad about this. He couldn't explain, could he? Staring out into the deepening dusk he saw, across the two driveways, that wash of light in the upper story. He stepped nimbly to his own back door and called, "Oh, Ralph, could you come here a minute?"

When Ralph came in, to be greeted with delight by Miggs (in whose opinion things were looking up), Howard was standing quietly by the sink. "I just saw something funny in your house. Same as I saw before. Come and look."

The older man was the shorter. He came up beside Howard. His head, at Howard's shoulder, was held in tension. Nothing happened for a moment or two.

"Well, I guess," said Howard, "it's like your tooth won't ache at the dentist's."

Then the light happened again.

Miggs began to bark suddenly. "Listen, Miggs, shut up, will you?" shouted Howard. Ralph was pushing against the sink. But his mood was not what Howard expected. "*You* saw something funny?" Ralph said firmly, when the dog was quiet. "*You're* not having hallucinations, are you? So whatever it was is real?"

"Whatever it is," said Howard cautiously.

But Ralph went rushing out the back door and Miggs tumbled after. Howard hurried to follow and saw the man jogging on the grass toward the candlelit picnic table with the dog bounding in pursuit.

Francine screamed in terror.

Howard swooped to catch the dog, and Stella began to soothe, and Ralph sat down.

When the noise and confusion had abated, Ralph said to his wife, "*He* just saw something funny. So now you tell *him* he's being haunted."

Francine began to cry. The oddest thing was that in the midst of her bawling she took up a piece of roll, buttered it, and stuffed it into her mouth.

"What's the matter?" cried Stella. "What did you see?"

"I don't know. Some car's headlight, maybe," said Ralph contemptuously, "but *she* says my house is haunted. She thinks we've got a ghost in there. Listen, I thought I heard something funny, a couple of times. But she didn't hear it, so she said that whatever is there must be haunting *me*. She said it must be Milly—Milly not wanting another woman in her house."

"Oh, come on," said Stella. "Really!" She was shocked, not so much by the idea of the supernatural as by the husband's ruthless betrayal of his wife.

"Well, I don't know." Francine was sobbing. "I don't know. I don't know."

Howard said, "Why don't we take Miggs over there? I told you, dogs can sense things out of our range. If *he* says it's okay, you can relax."

"No!" yelled Francine. She stood up. Her great bulk, in the growing darkness, was uncanny. "No!" she screamed. "I won't *have* a dog in the house. No!"

Miggs, who knew somehow that he was being insulted, replied in kind. So Howard dragged him back to his kitchen prison. What the hell, he was saying to himself. The worst of it was, he couldn't help thinking it might *be* hell.

The party was now definitely over. Francine kept blubbering and Ralph Sidwell was in a rage. He seemed to be a man who cast out whatever anger he felt, to ripple off on all sides, fall where it may. He seemed to be angry with the Lamboys. So the Sidwells went home.

Howard, stubborn to be kind whether they liked it or not, walked with them to the front sidewalk. Something made him say to them, "If you need any help, any time, just remember, will you? Here I am, right next door."

But they left without answering.

In the back yard Stella stood among the ruins. Howard went to let the dog out. Miggs raced around joyously for sixty seconds. He had been forgiven? That was fine with him. All was well.

But it wasn't.

The Lamboys ate dessert indoors. They didn't talk much. Stella could not be rid of the impression that somewhere beneath Francine's flesh there was a small, frail, and very frightened woman who had *not* been afraid of the dog. Stella was almost sure now that Francine hadn't wanted to come at all. But Ralph, unable to read the crooked signal of a false excuse, had fixed it so that she'd had to come. But what *was* she afraid of?

Howard kept wondering about the light, and what it had really been, and why Ralph had seemed, at first glad, and then angry, that somebody else had "seen something funny." What was Ralph afraid of?

Bedtime came and Howard let Miggs out briefly (no walk tonight), then checked the house and climbed upstairs. He went into their daughter's room that was always waiting for her, silent, vacant, but in sweet order. It was on the side toward the Sidwells. He looked out. The house over there had a light on somewhere—on the other side, downstairs—but as far as he could tell, all was peaceful.

Howard gave the whole thing up and dropped into bed.

At one o'clock in the morning the Lamboys' front doorbell rang and kept ringing in the manner that says *panic*. Howard leaped up, put on his robe and slippers, ran his hand over his rumpled hair, and went steadily down the stairs. Miggs, naturally, was curious too, and Howard could not but feel glad that the dog came to press his weight against his master's leg.

The porchlight fell on the white face of Ralph Sidwell. He was fully dressed. He said, "I'm afraid."

"What seems to be the trouble?" asked Howard quietly.

"I heard her scream. I think she— I don't— I'm afraid to go and see."

"Where is she?"

"Upstairs. I— Well, we had a fight. I couldn't— I didn't want to go up to bed. Then I heard the scream. I don't know what to do."

"I'll come with you," said Howard. "We'll take the dog. Let me get his leash."

Stella was halfway down the stairs and had heard. Howard snapped the leash on Miggs's collar. He took his flashlight, thinking of it vaguely as a weapon. But the weapon he relied on was the dog.

Ralph Sidwell could hardly stand on his puny legs. "I don't know if I c-can." His jaw shook.

Stella said, "We'll follow, Howard. You go and see." She bent in womanly compassion to this trouble. Howard walked toward whatever the trouble was, over there.

Strange night. The street was quiet. The little boxes stood in rows among the softly sighing trees, and how many civilizations—the insects, the little creeping creatures, the birds, the dogs and cats, and what others unknown—were coexisting all around the little boxes?

Howard went around the walks and up to his neighbor's box, the door of which stood wide open. He entered cautiously. The dog, keeping close, was silent.

He called out, "Francine? Francine?"

There was no answer. The lights were on in the living room to his right. The room was empty. The rest of the downstairs seemed dark and quiet. Howard led the dog toward other doors. He knew the floor plan. But Miggs made no sound.

So Howard started up the stairs. The dog, seeming nervous now, crowded him toward the railing. The upper-hall light switch was in a familiar place. Howard flicked it on and saw a pale blue mound on the floor.

Francine seemed neither conscious nor unconscious. She moaned but did not speak. She was bleeding from a scalp wound.

The ladder to the attic, that hinged from the hall ceiling, was down, and the square hole in the attic floor gaped open. Darkness lay beyond it. Howard's neck hair stirred. He didn't want to climb that ladder and turn his flashlight into that darkness. Wiser to check elsewhere first?

Now Miggs began to growl. Howard turned nervously and heard Stella's voice below. So he called down, "She's been hurt," keeping his voice not too loud, because more ears might be listening than he knew. "Not too badly, I think. Don't come up yet."

"Shall I call a doctor?" said his wife's clear voice.

"Good idea. Or else—no, wait."

Miggs was still growling and doing a kind of dance, advance and retreat, advance and retreat. "In here, eh?" said Howard to the dog. He pushed on the door of the back upstairs room that, in his house, was Stella's sewing room. It was a bedroom here.

Howard whipped the beam of his flashlight around the four walls. Nothing. No one. There was no clothes closet, so nobody could be hiding behind another door. Behind the door he'd come through? Howard shoved it flat against the wall. Nothing.

It was Miggs who saved his reason. (He said so later.)

Howard walked into the small room that seemed so empty. The dog went with him. But the dog *knew*. And the dog rushed and skittered, advanced and retreated, and his knowing muzzle, questing, knew *where*. So that when a hand of thin bone came out from under the bedspread's fringe and took Howard by the bare ankle, Howard did *not* fly up to the ceiling or out of his wits.

Oh, he jumped. But Miggs went at once into an uproar. So Howard, sheltered by the noise, dared to crouch and send light under the bed and into a face—a face the like of which he had never seen before.

"Guard. Stay," he said to Miggs, kindly but firmly. "Good boy. On guard."

He went into the hall. Francine, huge in her pale blue robe, had lifted herself on one arm; her other hand was on her bloody forehead. "Lester?" she piped.

Howard called down the stairs to Stella. "Call the police, hon. That's quickest." Then he looked at Francine.

"My baby? My boy?" said Francine, making everything a question, as if she were sure of nothing. "Never right? Nobody knew? Hungry? Ladder? Hit me?" Her bulk seemed to shake and then flow back down to the floor.

Stella was already on the phone. At the bottom of the stairs Ralph Sidwell was staring up at his neighbor.

"We have a problem here," said Howard quietly. "You've had a kind of stowaway, I think."

He went back to where Miggs was. The dog backed off, obeying. Slowly Howard persuaded the creature out from under the bed. A boy? Anywhere from fourteen to twenty-four. Who could say? He was deformed and stunted, wire-thin, incredibly pale, almost witless. He did not know how to stand up. He clung to the floor like a spider.

People came. . .

It was 3:30 in the morning when the Lamboys returned home at last. Stella said it was unthinkable to go to bed without breakfast and set to work creating homely scents of coffee and bacon.

Howard sat down on the dinette bench and Miggs jumped enthusiastically beside him. This was forbidden, but Howard was in no mood to scold.

"How did she ever sneak the Thing into the attic?" he said, because he was too filled with horror and pity to mention feelings: the brain was safer. "That's where the pillow was. She made a mistake about the quilt, eh? What do you know about that candle! Dangerous, whew! That alone!" (Alone, he thought, a living thing, ever alone, alone.) "She'd have to bring its food by night, on Sundays. But last night Ralph wouldn't go to bed. The ladder hit her."

Stella said sternly, "*Her* shame. So hide it and everything is dandy. And when the money is running out, go after some ordinary lonely man."

"What did *he* want? Home cooking?" said Howard as sternly as she. "How come he didn't notice this woman was sick and off the beam—*way* off, and so desperate. If it wasn't in his mind to pay any attention or to help her—"

In a moment Stella sat down and said, "If you're off, so far, and always getting farther, you'd have to have some little tiny pleasure. Something sweet in your mouth, at least?" She held her cheeks. They were feeling hollow.

Howard was thinking: In how many little boxes are there people, locked up, all alone, and in how many different ways? And how should we know? And what could we do? And why should that be?

Miggs was licking his master's left ear. We love. We love? And here we are together. So all is well. All is well?

Howard put his arm around the meat of Miggs, his warm loving creature who gave his heart in trust, even unto another species. "Miggs," he said, "what happens to people shouldn't happen to a dog." And he snuggled into the live fur.

by PATRICIA HIGHSMITH

THE EMPTY BIRDHOUSE

*Yes, in some indefinable way, we think there is an affinity
between Charlotte Armstrong's "The Light Next Door" and
Patricia Highsmith's "The Empty Birdhouse." But while
somewhere in the obscure creative origins of both stories
there is a basic idea in common, a conceptual sameness, you
will now discover one reason why the two stories turned out
to be so completely different. In Charlotte Armstrong's story,
as you now know, the Thing is not revealed until the end;
but in Patricia Highsmith's story the Thing is revealed at
the beginning. Both approaches are valid, and both produce
frissons d'horreur that will remain in your memory.*

*And both stories have something else in common. A trick
of the eye. A trick of the mind. And these tricks—do they expose or conceal the "many civilizations–the insects, the little
creeping creatures, the birds, the dogs and cats, and what
others unknown—coexisting all around the little boxes" we
call houses (quoted from Charlotte Armstrong's story)?
These tricks of the eye and the mind—do they expose or conceal "the dark and frightening gorge of the past," the guilts,
the crimes (quoted from Patricia Highsmith's story)? These
tricks of the eye and the mind—reader, beware . . .*

The first time Edith saw it she laughed, not believing
her eyes.

She stepped to one side and looked again; it was still
there, but a bit dimmer. A squirrel-like face—but demonic
in its intensity—looked out at her from the round hole in
the birdhouse. An illusion, of course, something to do with
shadows, or a knot in the wood of the back wall of the birdhouse. The sunlight fell plain on the six-by-nine-inch birdhouse in the corner made by the toolshed and the brick wall
of the garden. Edith went closer, until she was ten feet
away. The face disappeared.

That was funny, she thought as she went back into the

cottage. She would have to tell Charles tonight.

But she forgot to tell Charles.

Three days later she saw the face again. This time she was straightening up after having set two empty milk bottles on the back doorstep. A pair of beady black eyes looked out at her, straight and level, from the birdhouse, and they appeared to be surrounded by brownish fur. Edith flinched, then stood rigid. She thought she saw two rounded ears, a mouth that was neither animal nor bird, simply grim and cruel.

But she knew that the birdhouse was empty. The bluetit family had flown away weeks ago, and it had been a narrow squeak for the baby bluetits as the Masons' cat next door had been interested; the cat could reach the hole from the toolshed roof with a paw, and Charles had made the hole a trifle too big for bluetits. But Edith and Charles had staved Jonathan off until the birds were well away. Afterward, days later, Charles had taken the birdhouse down—it hung like a picture on a wire from a nail—and shaken it to make sure no debris was inside. Bluetits might nest a second time, he said. But they hadn't as yet—Edith was sure because she had kept watching.

And squirrels never nested in birdhouses. Or did they? At any rate, there were no squirrels around. Rats? They would never choose a birdhouse for a home. How could they get in anyway, without flying?

While these thoughts went through Edith's mind, she stared at the intense brown face, and the piercing black eyes stared back at her.

I'll simply go and see what it is, Edith thought, and stepped onto the path that led to the toolshed. But she went only three paces and stopped. She didn't want to touch the birdhouse and get bitten—maybe by a dirty rodent's tooth. She'd tell Charles tonight. But now that she was closer, the thing was still there, clearer than ever. It wasn't an optical illusion.

Her husband Charles Beaufort, a computing engineer, worked at a plant eight miles from where they lived. He frowned slightly and smiled when Edith told him what she had seen. "Really?" he said.

88

"I *may* be wrong. I wish you'd shake the thing again and see if there's anything in it," Edith said, smiling herself now, though her tone was earnest.

"All right, I will," Charles said quickly, then began to talk of something else. They were then in the middle of dinner.

Edith had to remind him when they were putting the dishes into the washing machine. She wanted him to look before it became dark. So Charles went out, and Edith stood on the doorstep, watching. Charles tapped on the birdhouse, listened with one ear cocked. He took the birdhouse down from the nail, shook it, then slowly tipped it so the hole was on the bottom. He shook it again.

"Absolutely nothing," he called to Edith. "Not even a piece of straw." He smiled broadly at his wife and hung the birdhouse back on the nail. "I wonder what you could've seen? You hadn't had a couple of Scotches, had you?"

"*No*. I described it to you." Edith felt suddenly blank, deprived of something. "It had a head a little larger than a squirrel's, beady black eyes, and a sort of serious mouth."

"Serious mouth!" Charles put his head back and laughed as he came back into the house.

"A tense mouth. It had a grim look," Edith said positively.

But she said nothing else about it. They sat in the living room, Charles looking over the newspaper, then opening his folder of reports from the office. Edith had a catalogue and was trying to choose a tile pattern for the kitchen wall. Blue and white, or pink and white and blue? She was not in a mood to decide, and Charles was never a help, always saying agreeably, "Whatever you like is all right with me."

Edith was 34. She and Charles had been married seven years. In the second year of their marriage Edith had lost the child she was carrying. She had lost it rather deliberately, being in a panic about giving birth. That was to say, her fall down the stairs had been rather on purpose, if she were willing to admit it, but the miscarriage had been put down as the result of an accident. She had never tried to have another child, and she and Charles had never even discussed it.

She considered herself and Charles a happy couple. Charles was doing well with Pan-Com Instruments, and they had more money and more freedom than several of their neighbors who were tied down with two or more children. They both liked entertaining, Edith in their house especially, and Charles on their boat, a thirty-foot motor launch which slept four. They plied the local river and inland canals on most weekends when the weather was good. Edith could cook amost as well afloat as on shore, and Charles obliged with drinks, fishing equipment and the record player. He would also dance a hornpipe on request.

During the weekend that followed—not a boating weekend because Charles had extra work—Edith glanced several times at the empty birdhouse, reassured now because she *knew* there was nothing in it. When the sunlight shone on it she saw nothing but a paler brown in the round hole, the back of the birdhouse; and when in shadow the hole looked black.

On Monday afternoon, as she was changing the bedsheets in time for the laundryman who came at three, she saw something slip from under a blanket that she picked up from the floor. Something ran across the floor and out the door—something brown and larger than a squirrel. Edith gasped and dropped the blanket. She tiptoed to the bedroom door, looked into the hall and on the stairs, the first five steps of which she could see.

What kind of animal made no noise at all, even on bare wooden stairs? Or had she really seen anything? But she was sure she had. She'd even had a glimpse of the small black eyes. It was the same animal she had seen looking out of the birdhouse.

The only thing to do was to find it, she told herself. She thought at once of the hammer as a weapon in case of need, but the hammer was downstairs. She took a heavy book instead and went cautiously down the stairs, alert and looking everywhere as her vision widened at the foot of the stairs.

There was nothing in sight in the living room. But it could be under the sofa or the armchair. She went into the kitchen and got the hammer from a drawer. Then she returned to the living room and shoved the armchair quickly some three feet. Nothing. She found she was afraid to bend down to look under the sofa, whose cover came almost to the floor, but she pushed it a few inches and listened.

It *might* have been a trick of her eyes, she supposed. Something like a spot floating before the eyes, after bending over the bed. She decided not to say anything to Charles about it. Yet in a way, what she had seen in the bedroom had been more definite than what she had seen in the birdhouse.

A baby yuma, she thought an hour later as she was sprinkling flour on a joint in the kitchen. A yuma. Now, where had that come from? Did such an animal exist? Had she seen a photograph of one in a magazine, or read the word somewhere?

Edith made herself finish all she intended to do in the kitchen, then went to the big dictionary and looked up the word yuma. It was not in the dictionary. A trick of her mind, she thought. Just as the animal was probably a trick of her eyes. But it was strange how they went together, as if the name were absolutely correct for the animal.

Two days later, as she and Charles were carrying their coffee cups into the kitchen, Edith saw it dart from under the refrigerator—or from behind the refrigerator—diagonally across the kitchen threshold and into the dining room. She almost dropped her cup and saucer, but caught them, and they chattered in her hands.

"What's the matter?" Charles asked.

"I saw it again!" Edith said. "The animal."

"What?"

"I didn't tell you," she began with a suddenly dry throat, as if she was making a painful confession. "I think I saw that thing—the thing that was in the birdhouse—upstairs in the bedroom on Monday. And I think I saw it again. Just now."

"Edith, my darling, there wasn't anything in the birdhouse."

"Not when you looked. But this animal moves quickly. It almost flies."

Charles's face grew more concerned. He looked where she was looking, at the kitchen threshold. "You saw it just now? I'll go look," he said, and walked into the dining room.

He gazed around on the floor, glanced at his wife, then rather casually bent and looked under the table, among the chair legs. "Really, Edith—"

"Look in the living room," Edith said.

Charles did, for perhaps fifteen seconds, then he came back, smiling a little. "Sorry to say this, old girl, but I think you're seeing things. Unless, of course, it was a mouse. We might have mice. I hope not."

"Oh, it's much bigger. And it's brown. Mice are gray."

"Yep," Charles said vaguely. "Well, don't worry, dear, it's not going to attack you. It's running." He added in a voice quite devoid of conviction, "If necessary, we'll get an exterminator."

"Yes," she said at once.

"How big is it?"

She held her hands apart at a distance of about sixteen inches. "This big."

"Sounds like it might be a ferret," he said.

"It's even quicker. And it has black eyes. Just now it stopped just for an instant and looked straight at me. Honestly, Charles." Her voice had begun to shake. She pointed to the spot by the refrigerator. "Just there it stopped for a split second and—"

"Edith, get a grip on yourself." He pressed her arm.

"It looks so evil. I can't tell you."

Charles was silent, looking at her.

"Is there any animal called a yuma?" she asked.

"A yuma? I've never heard of it. Why?"

"Because the name came to me today out of nowhere. I thought—because I'd thought of it and I'd never seen an animal like this that maybe I'd seen it somewhere."

"Y-u-m-a?"

Edith nodded.

Charles, smiling again because it was turning into a funny game, went to the dictionary as Edith had done and looked for the word. He closed the dictionary and went to the Encyclopaedia Britannica on the bottom shelves of the bookcase. After a minute's search he said to Edith, "Not in the dictionary and not in the Britannica either. I think it's a word you made up." And he laughed. "Or maybe it's a word in *Alice in Wonderland*."

It's a real word, Edith thought, but she didn't have the courage to say so. Charles would deny it.

Edith felt done in and went to bed around ten with her book. But she was still reading when Charles came in just before eleven. At that moment both of them saw it: it flashed from the foot of the bed across the carpet, in plain view of Edith and Charles, went under the chest of drawers and, Edith thought, out the door. Charles must have thought so, too, as he turned quickly to look into the hall.

"You saw it!" Edith said.

Charles's face was stiff. He turned the light on in the hall, looked, then went down the stairs.

He was gone perhaps three minutes, and Edith heard him pushing furniture about. Then he came back.

"Yes, I saw it." His face looked suddenly pale and tired.

But Edith sighed and almost smiled, glad that he finally believed her. "You see what I mean now. I wasn't seeing things."

"No," Charles agreed.

Edith was sitting up in bed. "The awful thing is, it looks uncatchable."

Charles began to unbutton his shirt. "Uncatchable. What a word. Nothing's uncatchable. Maybe it's a ferret. Or a squirrel."

"Couldn't you tell? It went right by you."

"Well!" He laughed. "It *was* pretty fast. You've seen it two or three times and you can't tell what it is."

"Did it have a tail? I can't tell if it had or if that's the whole body—that length."

Charles kept silent. He reached for his dressing gown, slowly put it on. "I think it's smaller than it looks. It is fast, so it seems elongated. Might be a squirrel."

"The eyes are in the front of its head. Squirrels' eyes are sort of at the side."

Charles stopped at the foot of the bed and looked under

it. He ran his hand over the tucked foot of the bed, underneath. Then he stood up. "Look, if we see it again—*if* we saw it—"

"What do you mean *if?* You did see it—you said so."

"I *think* so." Charles laughed. "How do I know my eyes or my mind isn't playing a trick on me? Your description was so eloquent." He sounded almost angry with her.

"Well—*if?*"

"If we see it again, we'll borrow a cat. A cat'll find it."

"Not the Masons' cat. I'd hate to ask them."

They had had to throw pebbles at the Masons' cat to keep it away when the bluetits were starting to fly. The Masons hadn't liked that. They were still on good terms with the Masons, but neither Edith nor Charles would have dreamed of asking to borrow Jonathan.

"We could call in an exterminator," Edith said.

"Ha! And what'll we ask him to look for?"

"What we saw," Edith said, annoyed because it was Charles who had suggested an exterminator just a couple of hours before. She was interested in the conversation, vitally interested, yet it depressed her. She felt it was vague and hopeless, and she wanted to lose herself in sleep.

"Let's try a cat," Charles said. "You know, Farrow has a cat. He got it from the people next door to him. You know, Farrow the accountant who lives on Shanley Road? He took the cat over when the people next door moved. But his wife doesn't like cats, he says. This one—"

"I'm not mad about cats either," Edith said. "We don't want to acquire a cat."

"No. All right. But I'm sure we could borrow this one, and the reason I thought of it is that Farrow says the cat's a marvelous hunter. It's a female nine years old, he says."

Charles came home with the cat the next evening, thirty minutes later than usual, because he had gone home with Farrow to fetch it. He and Edith closed the doors and the windows, then let the cat out of its basket in the living room. The cat was white with gray brindle markings, and a black tail. She stood stiffly, looking all around her with a glum and somewhat disapproving air.

"There, Puss-Puss," Charles said, stooping but not

touching her. "You're only going to be here a day or two. Have we got some milk, Edith? Or better yet, cream."

They made a bed for the cat out of a carton, put an old towel in it, then placed it in a corner of the living room, but the cat preferred the end of the sofa. She had explored the house perfunctorily and had shown no interest in the cupboards or closets, though Edith and Charles had hoped she would. Edith said she thought the cat was too old to be of much use in catching anything.

The next morning Mrs. Farrow rang up Edith and told her that they could keep Puss-Puss if they wanted to. "She's a clean cat and very healthy. I just don't happen to like cats. So if you take to her—or she takes to you—"

Edith wriggled out by an unusually fluent burst of thanks and explanations of why they had borrowed the cat, and she promised to ring Mrs. Farrow in a couple of days. Edith said she thought they had mice, but were not sure enough to call in an exterminator. This verbal effort exhausted her.

The cat spent most of her time sleeping either at the end of the sofa or on the foot of the bed upstairs, which Edith didn't care for but endured rather than alienate the cat. She even spoke affectionately to the cat and carried her to the open doors of closets, but Puss-Puss always stiffened slightly, not with fear but with boredom, and immediately turned away. Meanwhile she ate well of tuna, which the Farrows had prescribed.

Edith was polishing silver at the kitchen table on Friday afternoon when she saw the thing run straight beside her on the floor—from behind her, out the kitchen door into the dining room like a brown rocket. And she saw it turn to the right into the living room where the cat lay asleep.

Edith stood up at once and went to the living-room door. No sign of it now, and the cat's head still rested on her paws. The cat's eyes were closed. Edith's heart was beating fast. Her fear mingled with impatience and for an instant she experienced a sense of chaos and terrible disorder. The animal was in the room! And the cat was of no use at all! And the Wilsons were coming to dinner at seven o'clock. And she'd hardly have time to speak to Charles about it because he'd be washing and changing, and she couldn't, wouldn't mention it in front of the Wilsons, though they knew the Wilsons quite well. As Edith's chaos became frustration, tears burned her eyes. She imagined herself jumpy and awkward all evening, dropping things, and unable to say what was wrong.

"The yuma. The damned yuma!" she said softly and bitterly, then went back to the silver and doggedly finished polishing it and set the table.

The dinner, however, went quite well, and nothing was dropped or burned. Christopher Wilson and his wife Frances lived on the other side of the village, and had two boys, seven and five. Christopher was a lawyer for Pan-Com.

"You're looking a little peaked, Charles," Christopher said. "How about you and Edith joining us on Sunday?" He glanced at his wife. "We're going for a swim at Hadden and then for a picnic. Just us and the kids. Lots of fresh air."

"Oh—" Charles waited for Edith to decline, but she was silent. "Thanks very much. As for me—well, we'd thought of taking the boat somewhere. But we've borrowed a cat, and I don't think we should leave her alone all day."

"A cat?" asked Frances Wilson. "Borrowed it?"

"Yes. We thought we might have mice and wanted to find out," Edith put it with a smile.

Frances asked a question or two about the cat and the subject was dropped. Puss-Puss at the moment was upstairs, Edith thought. She always went upstairs when a new person came into the house.

Later when the Wilsons had left, Edith told Charles about seeing the animal again in the kitchen, and about the unconcern of Puss-Puss.

"That's the trouble. It doesn't make any noise," Charles said. Then he frowned. "Are you *sure* you saw it?"

"Just as sure as I am that I ever saw it," Edith said.

"Let's give the cat a couple of more days," Charles said.

The next morning, Saturday, Edith came downstairs around nine to start breakfast and stopped short at what she saw on the living-room floor. It was the yuma, dead, mangled at head and tail and abdomen. In fact, the tail was chewed off except for a damp stub about two inches long. And as for the head there was none. But the fur was brown, almost black where it was damp with blood.

Edith turned and ran up the stairs.

"Charles!"

He was awake, but sleepy. "What?"

"The cat caught it. It's in the living room. Come down, will you? —I can't face it, I really can't."

"Certainly, dear," Charles said, throwing off the covers.

He was downstairs a few seconds later. Edith followed him.

"Um. Pretty big," he said.

"What is it?"

"I dunno. I'll get the dustpan." He went into the kitchen.

Edith hovered, watching him push it onto the dustpan with a rolled newspaper. He peered at the gore, a chewed windpipe, bones. The feet had little claws.

"What is it? A ferret?" Edith asked.

"I dunno. I really don't." Charles wrapped the thing quickly in a newspaper. "I'll get rid of it in the ashcan. Monday's garbage day, isn't it?"

Edith didn't answer.

Charles went through the kitchen and she heard the lid of the ashcan rattle outside the kitchen door.

"Where's the cat?" she asked when he came in again.

He was washing his hands at the kitchen sink. "I don't know." He got the floor mop and brought it into the living room. He scrubbed the spot where the animal had lain. "Not much blood. I don't see any here, in fact."

While they were having breakfast, the cat came in through the front door, which Edith had opened to air the living room—although she had not noticed any smell. The cat looked at them in a tired way, barely raised her head, and said, "Mi-o-ow," the first sound she had uttered since her arrival.

"Good pussy!" Charles said with enthusiasm. "Good Puss-Puss!"

But the cat ducked from under his congratulatory hand that would have stroked her back and went on slowly into the kitchen for her breakfast of tuna.

Charles glanced at Edith with a smile which she tried to return. She had barely finished her egg, but could not eat a bite more of her toast.

She took the car and did her shopping in a fog, greeting familiar faces as she always did, yet she felt no contact between herself and other people. When she came home, Charles was lying on the bed, fully dressed, his hands behind his head.

"I wondered where you were," Edith said.

"I felt drowsy. Sorry." He sat up.

"Don't be sorry. If you want a nap, take one."

"I was going to get the cobwebs out of the garage and give it a good sweeping." He got to his feet. "But aren't you glad it's gone, dear—whatever it was?" he asked, forcing a laugh.

"Of course. Yes, God knows." But she still felt depressed, and she sensed that Charlie did, too. She stood hesitantly in the doorway. "I just wonder what it was." If we'd only see the head, she thought, but couldn't say it. Wouldn't the head turn up, inside or outside the house? The cat couldn't have eaten the skull.

"Something like a ferret," Charles said. "We can give the cat back now, if you like."

But they decided to wait till tomorrow to ring the Farrows.

Now Puss-Puss seemed to smile when Edith looked at her. It was a weary smile, or was the weariness only in the eyes? After all, the cat was nine. Edith glanced at the cat many times as she went about her chores that weekend. The cat had a different air, as if she had done her duty and knew it, but took no particular pride in it.

In a curious way Edith felt that the cat was in alliance with the yuma, or whatever animal it had been—was or had been in alliance. They were both animals and had understood each other, one the enemy and stronger, the other the prey. And the cat had been able to see it, perhaps hear it too, and had been able to get her claws into it. Above all, the cat was not afraid as she was, and even Charles was, Edith felt. At the same time she was thinking this, Edith realized that she disliked the cat. It had a gloomy, secretive look. The cat didn't really like them, either.

Edith had intended to phone the Farrows around three on Sunday afternoon, but Charles went to the telephone himself and told Edith he was going to call them. Edith dreaded hearing even Charles's part of the conversation, but she sat on with the Sunday papers on the sofa, listening.

Charles thanked them profusely and said the cat had caught something like a large squirrel or a ferret. But they really didn't want to keep the cat, nice as she was, and could they bring her over, say around six? "But—well, the job's done, you see, and we're awfully grateful. . .I'll definitely ask at the plant if there's anyone who'd like a nice cat."

Charles loosened his collar after he put the telephone down. "Whew! That was tough—I felt like a heel! But after all, there's no use saying we want the cat when we don't. Is there?"

"Certainly not. But we ought to take them a bottle of wine or something, don't you think?"

"Oh, definitely. What a good idea! Have we got any?"

They hadn't any. There was nothing in the way of unopened drink but a bottle of whiskey, which Edith proposed cheerfully.

"They did do us a big favor," Edith said.

Charles smiled. "That they did!" He wrapped the bottle in one of the green tissues in which their liquor store delivered bottles and set out with Puss-Puss in her basket.

Edith had said she did not care to go, but to be sure to give her thanks to the Farrows. Then Edith sat down on the sofa and tried to read the newspapers, but found her thoughts wandering. She looked around the empty, silent room, looked at the foot of the stairs and through the dining-room door.

It was gone now, the yuma baby. Why she thought it was a baby, she didn't know. A baby *what?* But she had always thought of it as young—and at the same time as cruel, and knowing about all the cruelty and evil in the world, the animal world and the human world. And its neck had been severed by a cat. They had not found the head.

She was still sitting on the sofa when Charles came back.

He came into the living room with a slow step and slumped into the armchair. "Well—they didn't exactly want to take her back."

"What do you mean?"

"It isn't their cat, you know. They only took her on out of kindness—or something—when the people next door left. They were going to Australia and couldn't take the cat with them. The cat sort of hangs around the two houses there, but the Farrows feed her. It's sad."

Edith shook her head involuntarily. "I really didn't like the cat. It's too old for a new home, isn't it?"

"I suppose so. Well, at least she isn't going to starve with the Farrows. Can we have a cup of tea, do you think? I'd rather have that than a drink."

And Charles went to bed early, after rubbing his right shoulder with liniment. Edith knew he was afraid of his bursitis or rheumatism starting.

"I'm getting old," Charles said to her. "Anyway, I feel old tonight."

So did Edith. She also felt melancholy. Standing at the bathroom mirror, she thought the little lines under her eyes looked deeper. The day had been a strain, for a Sunday. But the horror was out of the house. That was something. She had lived under it for nearly a fortnight.

Now that the yuma was dead, she realized what the trouble had been, or she could now admit it. The yuma had opened up the past, and it had been like a dark and frightening gorge. It had brought back the time when she had lost her child—on purpose—and it had recalled Charles's bitter chagrin then, his pretended indifference later. It had brought back her guilt. And she wondered if the animal had done the same thing to Charles? He hadn't been entirely noble in his early days at Pan-Com. He had told the truth about a man to a superior, the man had been dismissed—Charles had got his job—and the man had later committed suicide. Simpson. Charles had shrugged at the time. But had the yuma reminded him of Simpson? No person, no adult in the world, had a perfectly honorable past, a past without some crime in it. . .

Less than a week later, Charles was watering the roses one evening when he saw an animal's face in the hole of the birdhouse. It was the same face as the other animal's, or the face Edith had described to him, though he had never had such a good look at it as this.

There were the bright, fixed black eyes, the grim little mouth, the terrible alertness of which Edith had told him. The hose, forgotten in his hands, shot water straight out against the brick wall. He dropped the hose, and turned toward the house to cut the water off, intending to take the birdhouse down at once and see what was in it; but the birdhouse wasn't big enough to hold such an animal as Puss-Puss had caught. That was certain.

Charles was almost at the house, running, when he saw Edith standing in the doorway.

She was looking at the birdhouse. "There it is *again!*"

"Yes." Charles turned off the water. "This time I'll see what it is."

He started for the birdhouse at a trot, but midway he stopped, staring toward the gate.

Through the open iron gate came Puss-Puss, looking bedraggled and exhausted, even apologetic. She had been walking, but now she trotted in an elderly way toward Charles, her head hanging.

"She's back," Charles said.

A fearful gloom settled on Edith. It was all so ordained, so terribly predictable. There would be more and more yumas. When Charles shook the birdhouse in a moment, there wouldn't be anything in it, and then she would see the animal in the house, and Puss-Puss would again catch it. She and Charles, together, were stuck with it.

"She found her way all the way back here, I'm sure. Two miles," Charles said to Edith, smiling.

But Edith clamped her teeth to repress a scream.

by JULIAN SYMONS

'TWIXT THE CUP
AND THE LIP

*Mr. Rossiter Payne, a dignified and respected London busi-
nessman, was a part-time dealer in rare books and manuscripts. The rest of the time he was an unsuspected and undetected jewel thief. This year he was planning to give himself a truly splendid Christmas present—the mastermind's
share of the value of the Russian Royal Family Jewels. And,
as before in his successful criminal career, he planned the
coup with a professional's eye for every detail, especially the
vital element of synchronization. So nothing, of course,
could possibly go wrong—Mr. Rossiter Payne's plan was
foolproof, minutely dovetailed and jigsawed . . . An absorbing
novelet. . .*

"A beautiful morning, Miss Oliphant. I shall take a
short constitutional."

"Very well, Mr. Payne."

Mr. Rossiter Payne put on his good thick Melton overcoat, took his bowler hat off its peg, carefully brushed it,
and put it on. He looked at himself in a small glass and
nodded approvingly at what he saw.

He was a man in his early fifties, but he might have
passed for ten years less, so square were his shoulders, so
ruler-straight his back. Two fine wings of gray hair showed
under the bowler. He looked like a retired Guards officer,
although he had, in fact, no closer relationship with the
Army than an uncle who had been cashiered.

At the door he paused, his eyes twinkling. "Don't let
anybody steal the stock while I'm out, Miss Oliphant."

Miss Oliphant, a thin spinster of indeterminate middle-
age, blushed. She adored Mr. Payne.

He had removed his hat to speak to her. Now he clapped
it on his head again, cast an appreciative look at the bow

window of his shop, which displayed several sets of standard authors with the discreet legend above—*Rossiter Payne, Bookseller. Specialist in First Editions and Manuscripts*—and made his way up New Bond Street toward Oxford Street.

At the top of New Bond Street he stopped, as he did five days a week, at the stall on the corner. The old woman put the carnation into his buttonhole.

"Fourteen shopping days to Christmas now, Mrs. Shankly. We've all got to think about it, haven't we?"

A ten shilling note changed hands instead of the usual half crown. He left her blessing him confusedly.

This was perfect December weather—crisply cold, the sun shining. Oxford Street was wearing its holiday decorations—enormous gold and silver coins from which depended ropes of pearls, diamonds, rubies, emeralds. When lighted up in the afternoon they looked pretty, although a little garish for Mr. Payne's refined taste. But still, they had a certain symbolic feeling about them, and he smiled at them.

Nothing, indeed, could disturb Mr. Payne's good temper this morning—not the jostling crowds on the pavements or the customary traffic jams which seemed, indeed, to please him. He walked along until he came to a large store that said above it, in enormous letters, ORBIN'S. These letters were picked out in colored lights, and the lights themselves were festooned with Christmas trees and holly wreaths and the figures of the Seven Dwarfs, all of which lighted up.

Orbin's Department Store went right round the corner into the comparatively quiet Jessiter Street. Once again Mr. Payne went through a customary ceremony. He crossed the road and went down several steps into an establishment unique of its kind—Danny's Shoe Parlor. Here, sitting on a kind of throne in this semi-basement, one saw through a small window the lower halves of passers-by. Here Danny, with two assistants almost as old as himself, had been shining shoes for almost 30 years.

Leather-faced, immensely lined, but still remarkably sharp-eyed, Danny knelt down now in front of Mr. Payne, turned up the cuffs of his trousers, and began to put an altogether superior shine on already well-polished shoes.

"Lovely morning, Mr. Payne."

"You can't see much of it from here."

"More than you think. You see the pavements, and if they're not spotted, right off you know it isn't raining. Then there's something in the way people walk, you know what I mean, like it's Christmas in the air." Mr. Payne laughed indulgently. Now Danny was mildly reproachful. "You still haven't brought me in that pair of black shoes, sir."

Mr. Payne frowned slightly. A week ago he had been almost knocked down by a bicyclist, and the mudguard of the bicycle had scraped badly one of the shoes he was wearing, cutting the leather at one point. Danny was confident that he could repair the cut so that it wouldn't show. Mr. Payne was not so sure.

"I'll bring them along," he said vaguely.

"Sooner the better, Mr. Payne, sooner the better."

Mr. Payne did not like being reminded of the bicycle incident. He gave Danny half a crown instead of the ten shillings he had intended, crossed the road again, and walked into the side entrance of Orbin's, which called itself unequivocally "London's Greatest Department Store."

This end of the store was quiet. He walked up the stairs, past the Grocery Department on the ground floor, and Wine and Cigars on the second, to Jewelry on the third. There were rarely many people in this department, but today a small crowd had gathered around a man who was making a speech. A placard at the department entrance said: "The Russian Royal Family Jewels. On display for two weeks by kind permission of the Grand Duke and Grand Duchess of Moldo-Lithuania."

These were not the Russian Crown Jewels, seized by the Bolsheviks during the Revolution, but an inferior collection brought out of Russia by the Grand Duke and Grand Duchess, who had long since become plain Mr. and Mrs. Skandorski, who lived in New Jersey, and were now on a visit to England.

Mr. Payne was not interested in Mr. and Mrs. Skandorski, nor in Sir Henry Orbin who was stumbling through a short speech. He was interested only in the jewels. When the speech was over he mingled with the crowd round the showcase that stood almost in the middle of the room.

The royal jewels lay on beds of velvet—a tiara that looked too heavy to be worn, diamond necklaces and bracelets, a cluster of diamonds and emeralds, and a dozen other pieces, each with an elegant calligraphic description of its origin and history. Mr. Payne did not see the jewels as a romantic relic of the past, nor did he permit himself to think of them as things of beauty. He saw them as his personal Christmas present.

He walked out of the department, looking neither to left nor right, and certainly paying no attention to the spotty young clerk who rushed forward to open the door for him. He walked back to his bookshop, sniffing that sharp December air, made another little joke to Miss Oliphant, and told her she could go out to lunch. During her lunch hour he sold an American a set of a Victorian magazine called *The Jewel Box*.

It seemed a good augury.

In the past ten years Mr. Payne had engineered successfully—with the help of other, and inferior, intellects—six jewel robberies. He had remained undetected, he believed, partly because of his skill in planning, partly because he ran a perfectly legitimate book business, and partly because he broke the law only when he needed money. He had little interest in women, and his habits were generally ascetic, but he did have one vice.

Mr. Payne developed a system at roulette, an improvement on the almost infallible Frank-Konig system, and every year he went to Monte Carlo and played his system. Almost every year it failed—or rather, it revealed certain imperfections which he then tried to remedy.

It was to support his foolproof system that Mr. Payne had turned from bookselling to crime. He believed himself to be, in a quiet way, a mastermind in the modern criminal world.

Those associated with him were far from that, as he immediately would have acknowledged. He met them two evenings after he had looked at the royal jewels, in his pleasant little flat above the shop, which could be approached from a side entrance opening into an alley.

There was Stacey, who looked what he was, a thick-nosed thug; there was a thin young man in a tight suit whose name was Jack Line, and who was always called Straight or Straight Line; and there was Lester Jones, the spotty clerk in the Jewelry Department.

Stacey and Straight Line sat drinking whiskey, Mr. Payne sipped some excellent sherry, and Lester Jones drank nothing at all, while Mr. Payne in his pedantic, almost schoolmasterly manner, told them how the robbery was to be accomplished.

"You all know what the job is, but let me tell you how much it is worth. In its present form the collection is worth whatever sum you'd care to mention—a quarter of a million pounds perhaps. There is no real market value. But alas, it will have to be broken up. My friend thinks the value will be in the neighborhood of fifty thousand pounds. Not less, and not much more."

"Your friend?" the jewelry clerk said timidly.

"The fence, Lambie, isn't it?" It was Stacey who spoke. Mr. Payne nodded. "Okay, how do we split?"

"I will come to that later. Now, here are the difficulties. First of all, there are two store detectives on each floor. We must see to it that those on the third floor are not in the Jewelry Department. Next, there is a man named Davidson, an American, whose job it is to keep an eye on the jewels. He has been brought over here by a protection agency, and it is likely that he will carry a gun. Third, the jewels are in a showcase, and any attempt to open this showcase other than with the proper key will set off an alarm. The key is kept in the Manager's Office, inside the Jewelry Department."

Stacey got up, shambled over to the whiskey decanter, and poured himself another drink. "Where do you get all this from?"

Mr. Payne permitted himself a small smile. "Lester works in the department. Lester is a friend of mine."

Stacey looked at Lester with contempt. He did not like amateurs.

106

"Let me continue, and tell you how the obstacles can be overcome. First, the two store detectives. Supposing that a small fire bomb were planted in the Fur Department, at the other end of the third floor from Jewelry—that would certainly occupy one detective for a few minutes. Supposing that in the department that deals with ladies' hats, which is next to Furs, a woman shopper complained that she had been robbed—this would certainly involve the other store detective. Could you arrange this, Stace? These—assistants, shall I call them?—would be paid a straight fee. They would have to carry out their diversions at a precise time, which I have fixed as ten thirty in the morning."

"Okay," said Stacey. "Consider it arranged."

"Next, Davidson. He is an American, as I said, and Lester tells me that a happy event is expected in his family any day now. He has left Mrs. Davidson behind in America, of course. Now, supposing that a call came through, apparently from an American hospital, for Mr. Davidson. Supposing that the telephone in the Jewelry Department was out of order because the cord had been cut. Davidson would be called out of the department for the few minutes, no more, that we should need."

"Who cuts the cord?" Stacey asked.

"That will be part of Lester's job."

"And who makes the phone call?"

"Again, Stace, I hoped that you might be able to provide—"

"I can do that." Stacey drained his whiskey. "But what do you do?"

Mr. Payne's lips, never full, were compressed to a disapproving line. He answered the implied criticism only by inviting them to look at two maps—one the layout of the entire third floor, the other of the Jewelry Department itself. Stacey and Straight were impressed, as the uneducated always are, by such evidence of careful planning.

"The Jewelry Department is at one end of the third floor. It has only one exit—into the Carpet Department. There is a service lift which comes straight up into the Jewelry Department. You and I, Stace, will be in that. We shall stop it between floors with the Emergency Stop button. At exactly ten thirty-two we shall go up to the third floor. Lester will give us a sign. If everything has gone well, we proceed. If not, we call the job off. Now, what I propose. . . "

He told them, they listened, and they found it good. Even the ignorant, Mr. Payne was glad to see, could recognize genius. He told Straight Line his role.

"We must have a car, Straight, and a driver. What he has to do is simple, but he must stay cool. So I thought of you." Straight grinned.

"In Jessiter Street, just outside the side entrance to Orbin's, there is a parking space reserved for Orbin's customers. It is hardly ever full. But if it is full you can double park there for five minutes—cars often do that. I take it you can—acquire a car, shall I say?—for the purpose. You will face away from Oxford Street, and you will have no more than a few minutes' run to Lambie's house on Greenly Street. You will drop Stace and me, drive on a mile or two, and leave the car. We shall give the stuff to Lambie. He will pay on the nail. Then we all split."

From that point they went on to argue about the split. The argument was warm, but not really heated. They settled that Stacey would get 25 per cent of the total, Straight and Lester 12½ per cent each, and that half would go to the mastermind. Mr. Payne agreed to provide out of his share the £150 that Stacey said would cover the three diversions.

The job was fixed six days ahead—for Tuesday of the following week.

Stacey had two faults which had prevented him from rising high in his profession. One was that he drank too much, the other that he was stupid. He made an effort to keep his drinking under control, knowing that when he drank he talked. So he did not even tell his wife about the job, although she was safe enough.

But he could not resist cheating about the money, which Payne had given to him in full.

The fire bomb was easy. Stacey got hold of a little man named Shrimp Bateson, and fixed it with him. There was no risk, and Shrimp thought himself well paid with twenty-five quid. The bomb itself cost only a fiver, from a friend who dealt in hardware. It was guaranteed to cause just a little fire, nothing serious.

For the telephone call Stacey used a Canadian who was grubbing a living at a striptease club. It didn't seem to either of them that the job was worth more than a tenner, but the Canadian asked for twenty and got fifteen.

The woman was a different matter, for she had to be a bit of an actress, and she might be in for trouble since she actually had to cause a disturbance. Stacey hired an eighteen-stone Irish woman named Lucky O'Malley, who had once been a female wrestler, and had very little in the way of a record—nothing more than a couple of drunk and disorderlies. She refused to take anything less than £100, so that there was cash to spare. Stacey paid them all half their money in advance, put the rest of the £100 aside, and went on a roaring drunk for a couple of days, during which he somehow managed to keep his mouth buttoned and his nose clean.

When he reported on Monday night to Mr. Payne he seemed to have everything fixed, including himself.

Straight Line was a reliable character, a young man who kept himself to himself. He pinched the car on Monday afternoon, took it along to the semilegitimate garage run by his father-in-law, and put new license plates on it. There was no time for a respray job, but he roughed the car up a little so that the owner would be unlikely to recognize it if by an unlucky chance he should be passing outside Orbin's on Tuesday morning. During this whole operation, of course, Straight wore gloves.

He also reported to Mr. Payne on Monday night.

Lester's name was not really Lester—it was Leonard. His mother and his friends in Balham, where he had been born and brought up, called him Lenny. He detested this, as he detested his surname and the pimples that, in spite of his assiduous efforts with ointment, appeared on his face every couple of months. There was nothing he could do about the name of Jones, because it was on his National Insurance card, but Lester for Leonard was a gesture toward emancipation.

Another gesture was made when he left home and mother for a one-room flat in Notting Hill Gate. A third gesture—and the most important one—was his friendship with Lucille, whom he had met in a jazz club called The Whizz Fizz.

Lucille called herself an actress, but the only evidence of it was that she occasionally sang in the club. Her voice was tuneless, but loud. After she sang, Lester always bought her a drink, and the drink was always whiskey.

"So what's new?" she said. "Lester-boy, what's new?"

"I sold a diamond necklace today. Two hundred and fifty pounds. Mr. Marston was very pleased." Mr. Marston was the manager of the Jewelry Department.

"So Mr. Marston was pleased. Big deal." Lucille looked round restlessly, tapping her foot.

"He might give me a raise."

"Another ten bob a week and a pension for your fallen arches."

"Lucille, won't you—"

"No." The peak of emancipation for Lester, a dream beyond which his thoughts really could not reach, was that one day Lucille would come to live with him. Far from that, she had not even slept with him yet. "Look, Lesterboy, I know what I want, and let's face it, you haven't got it."

He was incautious enough to ask, "What?"

"Money, moolah, the green folding stuff. Without it you're nothing, with it they can't hurt you."

Lester was drinking whiskey too, although he didn't really like it. Perhaps but for the whiskey he would never have said, "Supposing I had money?"

"What money? Where would you get it—draw it out of the Savings Bank?"

"I mean a lot of money."

"Lester-boy, I don't think in penny numbers. I'm talking about real money."

The room was thick with smoke; the Whizz Fizz Kids were playing. Lester leaned back and said deliberately, "Next week I'll have money—thousands of pounds."

110

Lucille was about to laugh. Then she said, "It's my turn to buy a drink, I'm feeling generous. Hey, Joe. Two more of the same."

Later that night they lay on the bed in his one-room flat. She had let him make love to her, and he had told her everything.

"So the stuff's going to a man called Lambie in Greenly Street?"

Lester had never before drunk so much in one evening. Was it six whiskies or seven? He felt ill, and alarmed. "Lucille, you won't say anything? I mean, I wasn't supposed to tell—"

"Relax. What do you take me for?" She touched his cheek with red-tipped nails. "Besides, we shouldn't have secrets, should we?"

He watched her as she got off the bed and began to dress. "Won't you stay? I mean, it would be all right with the landlady."

"No can do, Lester-boy. See you at the club, though. Tomorrow night. Promise."

"Promise." When she had gone he turned over onto his side and groaned. He feared that he was going to be sick, and he was. Afterwards, he felt better.

Lucille went home to her flat in Earl's Court which she shared with a man named Jim Baxter. He had been sent to Borstal for a robbery from a confectioner's which had involved considerable violence. Since then he had done two short stretches. He listened to what she had to say, then asked, "What's this Lester like?"

"A creep."

"Has he got the nerve to kid you, or do you think it's on the level, what he's told you?"

"He wouldn't kid me. He wants me to live with him when he's got the money. I said I might."

Jim showed her what he thought of that idea. Then he said, "Tuesday morning, eh. Until then, you play along with this creep. Any change in plans I want to know about it. You can do it, can't you, baby?"

She looked up at him. He had a scar on the left side of his face which she thought made him look immensely attractive. "I can do it. And, Jim?"

"Yes?"

"What about afterwards?"

"Afterwards, baby? Well, for spending money there's no place like London. Unless it's Paris."

Lester Jones also reported on Monday night. Lucille was being very kind to him, so he no longer felt uneasy.

Mr. Payne gave them all a final briefing and stressed that timing, in this as in every similar affair, was the vital element.

Mr. Rossiter Payne rose on Tuesday morning at his usual time, just after eight o'clock. He bathed and shaved with care and precision, and ate his usual breakfast of one soft-boiled egg, two pieces of toast, and one cup of unsugared coffee. When Miss Oliphant arrived he was already in the shop.

"My dear Miss Oliphant. Are you, as they say, ready to cope this morning?"

"Of course, Mr. Payne. Do you have to go out?"

"I do. Something quite unexpected. An American collector named—but I mustn't tell his name even to you, he doesn't want it known—is in London, and he has asked me to see him. He wants to try to buy the manuscripts of—but there again I'm sworn to secrecy, although if I weren't I should surprise you. I am calling on him, so I shall leave things in your care until—" Mr. Payne looked at his expensive watch "—not later than midday. I shall certainly be back by then. In the meantime, Miss Oliphant, I entrust my ware to you."

She giggled. "I won't let anyone steal the stock, Mr. Payne."

Mr. Payne went upstairs again to his flat where, laid out on his bed, was a very different set of clothes from that which he normally wore. He emerged later from the little side entrance looking quite unlike the dapper, retired Guards officer known to Miss Oliphant.

His clothes were of the shabby nondescript ready-to-wear kind that might be worn by a City clerk very much down on his luck—the sleeve and trouser cuffs distinctly frayed, the tie a piece of dirty string. Curling strands of rather disgustingly gingery hair strayed from beneath his stained gray trilby hat and his face was gray too—gray and much lined, the face of a man of sixty who has been defeated by life.

Mr. Payne had bright blue eyes, but the man who came out of the side entrance had, thanks to contact lenses, brown ones. This man shuffled off down the alley with shoulders bent, carrying a rather dingy suitcase. He was quite unrecognizable as Rossiter Payne.

Indeed, if there was a criticism to be made of him, it was that he looked almost too much the "little man." Long, long ago, Mr. Payne had been an actor, and although his dramatic abilities were extremely limited, he had always loved and been extremely good at make-up.

He took with him a realistic-looking gun that, in fact, fired nothing more lethal than caps. He was a man who disliked violence, and thought it unnecessary.

After he left Mr. Payne on Monday night, Stacey had been unable to resist having a few drinks. The alarm clock wakened him to a smell of frizzling bacon. His wife sensed that he had a job on, and she came into the bedroom as he was taking the Smith and Wesson out of the cupboard.

"Bill." He turned round. "Do you need that?"

"What do you think?"

"Don't take it."

"Ah, don't be stupid."

"Bill, please. I get frightened."

Stacey put the gun into his hip pocket. "Won't use it. Just makes me feel a bit more comfortable, see?"

He ate his breakfast with a good appetite and then telephoned Shrimp Bateson, Lucy O'Malley, and the Canadian, to make sure they were ready. They were. His wife watched him fearfully. Then he came to say goodbye.

"Bill, look after yourself."

"Always do." And he was gone.

Lucille had spent Monday night with Lester. This was much against her wish, but Jim had insisted on it, saying that he must know of any possible last-minute change.

Lester had no appetite at all. She watched with barely concealed contempt as he drank no more than half a cup of coffee and pushed aside his toast. When he got dressed his fingers were trembling so, he could hardly button his shirt.

"Today's the day, then."

"Yes. I wish it was over."

"Don't worry."

He said eagerly, "I'll see you in the club tonight."

"Yes."

"I shall have the money then, and we could go away together. Oh, no, of course not—I've got to stay on the job."

"That's right," she said, humoring him.

As soon as he had gone, she rang Jim and reported there were no last-minute changes.

Straight Line lived with his family. They knew he had a job on, but nobody talked about it. Only his mother stopped him at the door and said, "Good luck, son," and his father said, "Keep your nose clean."

Straight went to the garage and got out the Jag.

10:30.

Shrimp Bateson walked into the Fur Department with a brown-paper package under his arm. He strolled about pretending to look at furs, while trying to find a place to put down the little parcel. There were several shoppers and he went unnoticed.

He stopped at the point where Furs led to the stairs, moved into a window embrasure, took the little metal cylinder out of its brown-paper wrapping, pressed the switch which started the mechanism, and walked rapidly away.

He had almost reached the door when he was tapped on the shoulder. He turned. A clerk was standing with the brown paper in his hand.

"Excuse me, sir, I think you've dropped something. I found this paper—"

"No, no," Shrimp said. "It's not mine."

There was no time to waste in arguing. Shrimp turned and half walked, half ran, through the doors and to the staircase. The clerk followed him. People were coming up

114

the stairs, and Shrimp, in a desperate attempt to avoid them, slipped and fell.

The clerk was standing hesitantly at the top of the stairs when he heard the *whoosh* of sound and, turning, saw flames. He ran down the stairs then, took Shrimp firmly by the arm and said, "I think you'd better come back with me, sir."

The bomb had gone off on schedule, setting fire to the window curtains and to one end of a store counter. A few women were screaming, and other clerks were busy saving the furs. Flack, one of the store detectives, arrived on the spot quickly, and organized the use of the fire extinguishers. They got the fire completely under control in three minutes.

The clerk, full of zeal, brought Shrimp along to Flack. "Here's the man who did it."

Flack looked at him. "Firebug, eh?"

"Let me go. I had nothing to do with it."

"Let's talk to the manager, shall we?" Flack said, and led Shrimp away.

The time was now 10:39.

Lucy O'Malley looked at herself in the glass, and at the skimpy hat perched on her enormous head. Her fake-crocodile handbag, of a size to match her person, had been put down on a chair nearby.

"What do you feel, madam?" the young saleswoman asked, ready to take her cue from the customer's reaction.

"Terrible."

"Perhaps it isn't really you."

"It looks bloody awful," Lucy said. She enjoyed swearing, and saw no reason why she should restrain herself.

The salesgirl laughed perfunctorily and dutifully, and moved over again toward the hats. She indicated a black hat with a wide brim. "Perhaps something more like this?"

Lucy looked at her watch. 10:31. It was time. She went across to her handbag, opened it, and screamed.

"Is something the matter, madam?"

"I've been robbed!"

"Oh, really, I don't think that can have happened."

Lucy had a sergeant-major's voice, and she used it. "Don't tell me what can and can't have happened, young woman. My money was in here, and now it's gone. Somebody's taken it."

The salesgirl, easily intimidated, blushed. The department supervisor, elegant, eagle-nosed, blue-rinsed, moved across like an arrow and asked politely if she could help.

"My money's been stolen," Lucy shouted. "I put my bag down for a minute, twenty pounds in it, and now it's gone. That's the class of people they get in Orbin's." She addressed this last sentence to another shopper, who moved away hurriedly.

"Let's look, shall we, just to make sure." Blue Rinse took hold of the handbag. Lucy took hold of it too, and somehow the bag's contents spilled onto the carpet.

"You stupid fool," Lucy roared.

"I'm sorry, madam," Blue Rinse said icily. She picked up handkerchief, lipstick, powder compact, tissues. Certainly there was no money in the bag. "You're sure the money was in the bag?"

"Of course I'm sure. It was in my purse. I had it five minutes ago. Someone here has stolen it."

"Not so loud, please, madam."

"I shall speak as loudly as I like. Where's your store detective, or haven't you got one?"

Sidley, the other detective on the third floor, was pushing through the little crowd that had collected. "What seems to be the matter?"

"This lady says twenty pounds has been stolen from her handbag." Blue Rinse just managed to refrain from emphasizing the word "lady."

"I'm very sorry. Shall we talk about it in the office?"

"I don't budge until I get my money back." Lucy was carrying an umbrella, and she waved it threateningly. However, she allowed herself to be led along to the office. There the handbag was examined again and the salesgirl, now tearful, was interrogated. There also Lucy, having surreptitiously glanced at the time, put a hand into the capacious pocket of her coat, and discovered the purse. There was twenty pounds in it, just as she had said.

She apologized, although the apology went much against the grain for her, declined the suggestion that she should return to the hat counter, and left the store with the consciousness of a job well done.

"Well," Sidley said. "I shouldn't like to tangle with her on a dark night."

The time was now 10:40.

The clock in the Jewelry Department stood at exactly 10:33 when a girl came running in, out of breath, and said to the manager, "Oh, Mr. Marston, there's a telephone call for Mr. Davidson. It's from America."

Marston was large, and inclined to be pompous. "Put it through here, then."

"I can't. There's something wrong with the line in this department—it seems to be dead."

Davidson had heard his name mentioned, and came over to them quickly. He was a crew-cut American, tough and lean. "It'll be about my wife, she's expecting a baby. Where's the call?"

"We've got it in Administration, one floor up."

"Come on, then." Davidson started off at what was almost a run, and the girl trotted after him. Marston stared at both of them disapprovingly. He became aware that one of his clerks, Lester Jones, was looking rather odd.

"Is anything the matter, Jones? Do you feel unwell?"

Lester said that he was all right. The act of cutting the telephone cord had filled him with terror, but with the departure of Davidson he really did feel better. He thought of the money—and of Lucille.

Lucille was just saying goodbye to Jim Baxter and his friend Eddie Grain. They were equipped with an arsenal of weapons, including flick knives, bicycle chains, and brass knuckles. They did not, however, carry revolvers.

"You'll be careful," Lucille said to Jim.

"Don't worry. This is going to be like taking candy from a baby, isn't it, Eddie?"

"S'right," Eddie said. He had a limited vocabulary, and an almost perpetual smile. He was a terror with a knife. . .

The Canadian made the call from the striptease club. He had a girl with him. He had told her that it would be a big giggle. When he heard Davidson's voice—the time was just after ten thirty-four—he said, "Is that Mr. Davidson?"

"Yes."

"This is the James Long Foster Hospital in Chicago, Mr. Davidson, Maternity Floor."

"Yes?"

"Will you speak up, please. I can't hear you very well."

"Have you got some news of my wife?" Davidson said loudly. He was in a small booth next to the store switchboard. There was no reply. "Hello?"

The Canadian put one hand over the receiver, and ran the other up the girl's bare thigh. "Let him stew a little." The girl laughed. They could hear Davidson asking if they were still on the line. Then the Canadian spoke again.

"Hello, hello, Mr. Davidson. We seem to have a bad connection."

"I can hear you clearly. What news is there?"

"No need to worry, Mr. Davidson. Your wife is fine."

"Has she had the baby?"

The Canadian chuckled. "Now, don't be impatient. That's not the kind of thing you can hurry, you know."

"What have you got to tell me then? Why are you calling?"

The Canadian put his hand over the receiver again, said to the girl, "You say something."

"What shall I say?"

"Doesn't matter—that we've got the wires crossed or something."

The girl leaned over, picked up the telephone. "This is the operator. Who are you calling?"

In the telephone booth sweat was running off Davidson. He hammered with his fist on the wall of the booth. "Damn you, get off the line! Put me back to the Maternity Floor."

"This is the operator. Who do you want, please?"

Davidson checked himself suddenly. The girl had a Cockney voice. "Who are you? What's your game?"

The girl handed the telephone back to the Canadian, looking frightened. "He's on to me."

"Hell." The Canadian picked up the receiver again, but the girl had left it uncovered, and Davidson had heard the girl's words. He dropped the phone, pushed open the door of the booth, and raced for the stairs. As he ran he loosened the revolver in his hip pocket.

The time was now 10:41.

Straight Line brought the Jaguar smoothly to a stop in the space reserved for Orbin's customers, and looked at his watch. It was 10:31.

Nobody questioned him, nobody so much as gave him a glance. Beautiful, he thought, a nice smooth job, really couldn't be simpler. Then his hands tightened on the steering wheel.

He saw in the rear-view mirror, standing just a few yards behind him, a policeman. Three men were evidently asking the policeman for directions, and the copper was consulting a London place map.

Well, Straight thought, he can't see anything of me except my back, and in a couple of minutes he'll be gone. There was still plenty of time. Payne and Stacey weren't due out of the building until 10:39 or 10:40. Yes, plenty of time.

But there was a hollow feeling in Straight's stomach as he watched the policeman in his mirror.

Some minutes earlier, at 10:24, Payne and Stacey had met at the service elevator beside the Grocery Department on the ground floor. They had met this early because of the possibility that the elevator might be in use when they needed it, although from Lester's observation it was used mostly in the early morning and late afternoon.

They did not need the elevator until 10:30, and they would be very unlucky if it was permanently in use at that time. If they were that unlucky—well, Mr. Payne had said with the pseudo-philosophy of the born gambler, they would have to call the job off. But even as he said this he knew that it was not true, and that having gone so far he would not turn back.

The two men did not speak to each other, but advanced steadily toward the elevator by way of inspecting chow mein, hymettus honey, and real turtle soup. The Grocery Department was full of shoppers, and the two men were quite unnoticed. Mr. Payne reached the elevator first and pressed the button. They were in luck. The door opened.

Within seconds they were both inside. Still neither man spoke. Mr. Payne pressed the button which said 3, and then, when they had passed the second floor, the button that said Emergency Stop. Jarringly the elevator came to a stop. It was now immobilized, so far as a call from outside was concerned. It could be put back into motion only by calling in engineers who would free the Emergency Stop mechanism—or, of course, by operating the elevator from inside.

Stacey shivered a little. The elevator was designed for freight, and therefore roomy enough to hold twenty passengers; but Stacey had a slight tendency to claustrophobia which was increased by the thought that they were poised between floors. He said, "I suppose that bloody thing will work when you press the button?"

"Don't worry, my friend. Have faith in me." Mr. Payne opened the dingy suitcase, revealing as he did so that he was now wearing rubber gloves. In the suitcase were two long red cloaks, two fuzzy white wigs, two thick white beards, two pairs of outsize horn-rimmed spectacles, two red noses, and two hats with large tassels. "This may not be a perfect fit for you, but I don't think you can deny that it's a perfect disguise."

They put on the clothes, Mr. Payne with the pleasure he always felt in dressing up, Stacey with a certain reluctance. The idea was clever, all right, he had to admit that, and when he looked in the elevator's small mirror and saw a Santa Claus looking back at him, he was pleased to find himself totally unrecognizable. Deliberately he took the Smith and Wesson out of his jacket and put it into the pocket of the red cloak.

"You understand, Stace, there is no question of using that weapon."

"Unless I have to."

"There is no question," Mr. Payne repeated firmly. "Violence is never necessary. It is a confession that one lacks intelligence."

"We got to point it at them, haven't we? Show we mean business."

Mr. Payne acknowledged that painful necessity by a downward twitch of his mouth, undiscernible beneath the false beard.

"Isn't it time yet?"

Mr. Payne looked at his watch. "It is now ten twenty-nine. We go—over the top, you might call it—at ten thirty-two precisely. Compose yourself to wait, Stace."

Stacey grunted. He could not help admiring his companion, who stood peering into the small glass, adjusting his beard and mustache, and settling his cloak more comfortably. When at last Mr. Payne nodded, and said, "Here we go," and pressed the button marked 3, resentment was added to admiration. He's all right now, but wait till we get to the action, Stacey thought. His gloved hand on the Smith and Wesson reassured him of strength and efficiency.

The elevator shuddered, moved upward, stopped. The door opened. Mr. Payne placed his suitcase in the open elevator door so that it would stay open and keep the elevator at the third floor. Then they stepped out.

To Lester the time that passed after Davidson's departure and before the elevator door opened was complete and absolute torture.

The whole thing had seemed so easy when Mr. Payne had outlined it to them. "It is simply a matter of perfect timing," he had said. "If everybody plays his part properly, Stace and I will be back in the lift within five minutes. Planning is the essence of this, as of every scientific operation. Nobody will be hurt, and nobody will suffer financially except"—and here he had looked at Lester with a twinkle in his frosty eyes—"except the insurance company. And I don't think the most tenderhearted of us will worry too much about the insurance company."

That was all very well, and Lester had done what he was supposed to do, but he hadn't really been able to believe that the rest of it would happen. He had been terrified, but with the terror was a mixed sense of unreality.

He still couldn't believe, even when Davidson went to the telephone upstairs, that the plan would go through without a hitch. He was showing some costume jewelry to a thin old woman who kept roping necklaces around her scrawny neck, and while he did so he kept looking at the elevator, above which was the department clock. The hands moved slowly, after Davidson left, from 10:31 to 10:32.

They're not coming, Lester thought. It's all off. A flood of relief, touched with regret but with relief predominating, went through him. Then the elevator door opened, and the two Santa Clauses stepped out. Lester started convulsively.

"Young man," the thin woman said severely, "it doesn't seem to me that I have your undivided attention. Haven't you anything in blue and amber?"

It had been arranged that Lester would nod to signify that Davidson had left the department, or shake his head if anything had gone wrong. He nodded now as though he had St. Vitus's Dance.

The thin woman looked at him, astonished. "Young man, is anything the matter?"

"Blue and amber," Lester said wildly, "amber and blue." He pulled out a box from under the counter and began to look through it. His hands were shaking.

Mr. Payne had been right in his assumption that no surprise would be occasioned by the appearance of two Santa Clauses in any department at this time of year. This, he liked to think, was his own characteristic touch—the touch of, not to be unduly modest about it, creative genius. There were a dozen people in the Jewelry Department, half of them looking at the Russian Royal Family Jewels, which had proved less of an attraction than Sir Henry Orbin had hoped. Three of the others were wandering about in the idle way of people who are not really intending to buy anything, and the other three were at the counters, where they were being attended to by Lester, a salesgirl whose name was Miss Glenny, and by Marston himself.

The appearance of the Santa Clauses aroused only the feeling of pleasure experienced by most people at sight of these slightly artificial figures of jollity. Even Marston barely glanced at them. There were half a dozen Santa Clauses in the store during the weeks before Christmas, and he assumed that these two were on their way to the Toy Department, which was also on the third floor, or to Robin Hood in Sherwood Forest tableau, which was this year's display for children.

The Santa Clauses walked across the floor together as though they were in fact going into Carpets and then on to the Toy Department, but after passing Lester they diverged. Mr. Payne went to the archway that led from Jewelry to Carpets, and Stacey abruptly turned behind Lester toward the Manager's Office.

Marston, trying to sell an emerald brooch to an American who was not at all sure his wife would like it, looked up in surprise. He had a natural reluctance to make a fuss in public, and also to leave his customer; but when he saw Stacey with a hand actually on the door of his own small but sacred office he said to the American, "Excuse me a moment, sir," and said to Miss Glenny, "Look after this gentleman, please"—by which he meant that the American should not be allowed to walk out with the emerald brooch—and called out, although not so loudly that the call could be thought of as anything so vulgar as a shout, "Just a moment, please. What are you doing there? What do you want?"

Stacey ignored him. In doing so he was carrying out Mr. Payne's specific instructions. At some point it was inevitable that the people in the department would realize that a theft was taking place, but the longer they could be kept from realizing it, Mr. Payne had said, the better. Stacey's own inclination would have been to pull out his revolver at once and terrorize anybody likely to make trouble; but he did as he was told.

The Manager's Office was not much more than a cubbyhole, with papers neatly arranged on a desk; behind the desk, half a dozen keys were hanging on the wall. The showcase key, Lester had said, was the second from the left, but for the sake of appearances Stacey took all the keys. He had just turned to go when Marston opened the door and saw the keys in Stacey's hand.

The manager was not lacking in courage. He understood at once what was happening and, without speaking, tried to grapple with the intruder. Stacey drew the Smith and Wesson from his pocket and struck Marston hard with it on the forehead. The manager dropped to the ground. A trickle of blood came from his head.

The office door was open, and there was no point in making any further attempt at deception. Stacey swung the revolver around and rasped, "Just keep quiet, and nobody else will get hurt."

Mr. Payne produced his cap pistol and said, in a voice as unlike his usual cultured tones as possible, "Stay where you are. Don't move. We shall be gone in five minutes."

Somebody said, "Well, I'm damned." But no one moved. Marston lay on the floor, groaning. Stacey went to the showcase, pretended to fumble with another key, then inserted the right one. The case opened at once. The jewels lay naked and unprotected. He dropped the other keys on the floor, stretched in his gloved hands, picked up the royal jewels, and stuffed them into his pocket.

It's going to work, Lester thought unbelievingly, it's going to work. He watched, fascinated, as the cascade of shining stuff vanished into Stacey's pocket. Then he became aware that the thin woman was pressing something into his hand. Looking down, he saw with horror that it was a large, brand-new clasp knife, with the dangerous-looking blade open.

"Bought it for my nephew," the thin woman whispered. "As he passes you, go for him."

It had been arranged that if Lester's behavior should arouse the least suspicion he should make a pretended attack on Stacey, who would give him a punch just severe enough to knock him down. Everything had gone so well, however, that this had not been necessary, but now it seemed to Lester that he had no choice.

As the two Santa Clauses backed across the room toward the service elevator, covering the people at the counters with their revolvers, one real and the other a toy, Lester launched himself feebly at Stacey, with the clasp knife demonstratively raised. At the same time Marston, on the other side of Stacey and a little behind him, rose to his feet and staggered in the direction of the elevator.

Stacey's contempt for Lester increased with the sight of the knife, which he regarded as an unnecessary bit of bravado. He shifted the revolver to his left hand, and with his right punched Lester hard in the stomach. The blow doubled Lester up. He dropped the knife and collapsed to the floor, writhing in quite genuine pain.

The delivery of the blow delayed Stacey so that Marston was almost up to him. Mr. Payne, retreating rapidly to the elevator, shouted a warning, but the manager was on Stacey, clawing at his robes. He did not succeed in pulling off the red cloak, but his other hand came away with the wig, revealing Stacey's own cropped brown hair. Stacey snatched back the wig, broke away, and fired the revolver with his left hand.

Perhaps he could hardly have said himself whether he intended to hit Marston, or simply to stop him. The bullet missed the manager and hit Lester, who was rising on one knee. Lester dropped again. Miss Glenny screamed, another woman cried out, and Marston halted.

Mr. Payne and Stacey were almost at the elevator when Davidson came charging in through the Carpet Department entrance. The American drew the revolver from his pocket and shot, all in one swift movement. Stacey fired back wildly. Then the two Santa Clauses were in the service elevator, and the door closed on them.

Davidson took one look at the empty showcase, and shouted to Marston, "Is there an emergency alarm that rings downstairs?"

The manager shook his head. "And my telephone's not working."

"They've cut the line." Davidson raced back through the Carpet Department to the passenger elevators.

Marston went over to where Lester was lying, with half a dozen people round him, including the thin woman. "We must get a doctor."

The American he had been serving said, "I am a doctor." He was bending over Lester, whose eyes were wide open.

"How is he?"

The American lowered his voice. "He got it in the abdomen."

Lester seemed to be trying to raise himself up. The thin woman helped him. He sat up, looked around, and said, "Lucille." Then blood suddenly rushed out of his mouth.

The doctor bent over again, then looked up. "He's dead."

The thin woman gave Lester a more generous obituary than he deserved. "He wasn't a very good clerk, but he was a brave young man."

Straight Line, outside in the stolen Jag, waited for the policeman to move. But not a bit of it. The three men with the policeman were pointing to a particular spot on the map, and the copper was laughing; they were having some sort of stupid joke together. What the hell, Straight thought, hasn't the bleeder got any work to do, doesn't he know he's not supposed to be hanging about? Why doesn't he move on?

Straight looked at his watch. 10:34, coming up to 10:35—and now, as the three men finally moved away, what should happen but that a teen-age girl should come up, and the copper was bending over toward her with a look of holiday good-will.

It's no good, Straight thought, I shall land them right in his lap if I stay here. He pulled away from the parking space, looked again at his watch. He was obsessed by the need to get out of the policeman's sight.

Once round the block, he thought, just once round can't take more than a minute, and I've got more than two minutes to spare. Then if the stupid copper's still here when I come back, I'll stay a few yards away from him with my engine running.

He moved down Jessiter Street and a moment after Straight had gone, the policeman, who had never even glanced at him, moved away too.

By Mr. Payne's plan they should have taken off their Santa Claus costumes in the service elevator and walked out at the bottom as the same respectable, anonymous citizens who had gone in; but as soon as they were inside the

126

elevator Stacey said, "He hit me." A stain showed on the scarlet right arm of his robe.

Mr. Payne pressed the button to take them down. He was proud that, in this emergency, his thoughts came with clarity and logic. He spoke them aloud.

"No time to take these off. Anyway, they're just as good a disguise in the street. Straight will be waiting. We step out and into the car, take them off there. Davidson shouldn't have been back in that department for another two minutes."

"I gotta get to a doctor."

"We'll go to Lambie's first. He'll fix it." The elevator whirred downward. Almost timidly, Mr. Payne broached the subject that worried him most. "What happened to Lester?"

"He caught one." Stacey was pale.

The elevator stopped. Mr. Payne adjusted the wig on Stacey's head. "They can't possibly be waiting for us, there hasn't been time. We just walk out. Not too fast, remember. Casually, normally."

The elevator door opened and they walked the fifty feet to the Jessiter Street exit. They were delayed only by a small boy who rushed up to Mr. Payne, clung to his legs and shouted that he wanted his Christmas present. Mr. Payne gently disengaged him, whispered to his mother, "Our tea break. Back later," and moved on.

Now they were outside in the street. But there was no sign of Straight or the Jaguar.

Stacey began to curse. They crossed the road from Orbin's, stood outside Danny's Shoe Parlor for a period that seemed to both of them endless, but was, in fact, only thirty seconds. People looked at them curiously—two Santa Clauses wearing false noses—but they did not arouse great attention. They were oddities, yes, but oddities were in keeping with the time of year and Oxford Street's festive decorations.

"We've got to get away," Stacey said. "We're sitting ducks."

"Don't be a fool. We wouldn't get a hundred yards."

"Planning," Stacey said bitterly. "Fine bloody planning. If you ask me—"

"Here he is."

The Jag drew up beside them, and in a moment they were in and down Jessiter Street, away from Orbin's. Davidson was on the spot less than a minute later, but by the time he had found passers-by who had seen the two Santa Clauses get into the car, they were half a mile away.

Straight Line began to explain what had happened, Stacey swore at him, and Mr. Payne cut them both short.

"No time for that. Get these clothes off, talk later."

"You got the rocks?"

"Yes, but Stace has been hit. By the American detective. I don't think it's bad, though."

"Whatsisname, Lester, he okay?"

"There was trouble. Stace caught him with a bullet."

Straight said nothing more. He was not one to complain about something that couldn't be helped. His feelings showed only in the controlled savagery with which he maneuvered the Jag.

While Straight drove, Mr. Payne was taking off his own Santa Claus outfit and helping Stacey off with his. He stuffed them, with the wigs and beards and noses, back into the suitcase. Stacey winced as the robe came over his right arm, and Mr. Payne gave him a handkerchief to hold over it. At the same time he suggested that Stacey hand over the jewels, since Mr. Payne would be doing the negotiating with the fence. It was a mark of the trust that both men still reposed in Mr. Payne that Stacey handed them over without a word, and that Straight did not object or even comment.

They turned into the quiet Georgian terrace where Lambie lived. "Number fifteen, righthand side," Mr. Payne said.

Jim Baxter and Eddie Grain had been hanging about in the street for several minutes. Lucille had learned from Lester what car Straight was driving. They recognized the Jag immediately, and strolled toward it. They had just reached the car when it came to a stop in front of Lambie's house. Stacey and Mr. Payne got out.

Jim and Eddie were not, after all, too experienced. They made an elementary mistake in not waiting until Straight had driven away. Jim had his flick knife out and was pointing it at Mr. Payne's stomach.

"Come on now, dad, give us the stuff and you won't get hurt," he said.

On the other side of the car Eddie Grain, less subtle, swung at Stacey with a shortened length of bicycle chain. Stacey, hit round the head, went down, and Eddie was on top of him, kicking, punching, searching.

Mr. Payne hated violence, but he was capable of defending himself. He stepped aside, kicked upward, and knocked the knife flying from Jim's hand. Then he rang the doorbell of Lambie's house. At the same time Straight got out of the car and felled Eddie Grain with a vicious rabbit punch.

During the next few minutes several things happened simultaneously. At the end of the road a police whistle was blown, loudly and insistently, by an old lady who had seen what was going on. Lambie, who also saw what was going on and wanted no part of it, told his manservant on no account to answer the doorbell or open the door.

Stacey, kicked and beaten by Eddie Grain, drew his revolver and fired four shots. One of them struck Eddie in the chest, and another hit Jim Baxter in the leg. Eddie scuttled down the street holding his chest, turned the corner, and ran slap into the arms of two policemen hurrying to the scene.

Straight, who did not care for shooting, got back into the Jag and drove away. He abandoned the Jag as soon as he could, and went home.

When the police arrived, with a bleeding Eddie in tow, they found Stacey and Jim Baxter on the ground, and several neighbors only too ready to tell confusing stories about the great gang fight that had just taken place. They interrogated Lambie, of course, but he had not seen or heard anything at all.

And Mr. Payne? With a general melee taking place, and

Lambie clearly not intending to answer his doorbell, he had walked away down the road. When he turned the corner he found a cab, which he took to within a couple of hundred yards of his shop. Then, an anonymous man carrying a shabby suitcase, he went in through the little side entrance.

Things had gone badly, he reflected as he again became Mr. Rossiter Payne the antiquarian bookseller, mistakes had been made. But happily they were not his mistakes. The jewels would be hot, no doubt; they would have to be kept for a while, but all was not lost.

Stace and Straight were professionals—they would never talk. And although Mr. Payne did not, of course, know that Lester was dead, he realized that the young man would be able to pose as a wounded hero and was not likely to be subjected to severe questioning.

So Mr. Payne was whistling as he went down to greet Miss Oliphant.

"Oh, Mr. Payne," she trilled. "You're back before you said. It's not half past eleven."

Could that be true? Yes, it was.

"Did the American collector—I mean, will you be able to sell him the manuscripts?"

"I hope so. Negotiations are proceeding, Miss Oliphant."

The time passed uneventfully until 2:30 in the afternoon when Miss Oliphant entered his little private office. "Mr. Payne, there are two gentlemen to see you. They won't say what it's about, but they look—well, rather funny."

As soon as Mr. Payne saw them and even before they produced their warrant cards, he knew that there was nothing funny about them. He took them up to the flat and tried to talk his way out of it, but he knew it was no use. They hadn't yet got search warrants, the Inspector said, but they would be taking Mr. Payne along anyway. It would save them some trouble if he would care to show them—"

Mr. Payne showed them. He gave them the jewels and the Santa Claus disguises. Then he sighed at the weakness of subordinates. "Somebody squealed, I suppose."

"Oh, no. I'm afraid the truth is you were a bit careless."

"*I* was careless?" Mr. Payne was genuinely scandalized.

"Yes. You were recognized."

"Impossible!"

"Not at all. When you left Orbin's and got out into the street, there was a bit of a mixup so that you had to wait. Isn't that right?"

"Yes, but I was completely disguised."

"Danny the shoeshine man knows you by name, doesn't he?"

"Yes, but he couldn't possibly have seen me."

"He didn't need to. Danny can't see any faces from his basement, as you know, but he did see something, and he came to tell us about it. He saw two pairs of legs, and the bottoms of some sort of red robes. And he saw the shoes. He recognized one pair of shoes, Mr. Payne. Not those you're wearing now, but that pair on the floor over there."

Mr. Payne looked across the room at the black shoes—shoes so perfectly appropriate to the role of shabby little clerk that he had been playing, and at the decisive, fatally recognizable sharp cut made by the bicycle mudguard in the black leather.

by **JOHN LUTZ**

THE INSOMNIACS CLUB

*There are day people and there are night people, and as the
founder and unofficial president of The Insomniacs Club
pointed out: night people have certain definite advantages...a clever and "different" story...*

Walter Thorn's rubbersoled shoes trod silently on the
shadowed pavement. He looked about him, his slen-
der face under the thinning brown hair its usual combination of intensity and frustration. There should be noise, he
thought, as he gazed at the rows of tall brick buildings that
towered into the darkness on either side of him. He was
walking at the bottom of an immense stone canyon, a place
of hollow echoes, but it was 3 A.M. and there simply was no
noise to create echoes. The only thing stirring was Walter,
and it seemed to him that his passage down North Street
was like his passage through life—silent, unnoticed, mean-
ingless.

He reached beneath his jacket and drew a pack of
cigarettes from the breast pocket of his pajamas. Yes, he
thought again—for he was prone to daydreams if not night
dreams—if I were a motion picture director I'd have noise
here, maybe a far-off police siren, an ashcan lid falling,
hollow footsteps . . . He flicked his lighter and slid it back
into his pants pocket. He wasn't a motion picture director,
of course; he was an accountant—had been for ten years, at
the same firm, and for almost the same salary.

He drew on the cigarette and resumed his walk in the
night. There was a dreamlike, treadmill quality to walking
through the Sterling Executive Apartment project, for all
the buildings were alike, neat four-story brick moderns.
And you could walk six blocks in any direction from Walter's building before seeing anything different. Walter had
lived here for almost a year now, at his wife's insistence.
Lately he did everything at Beulah's insistence.

Walter's step faltered for a moment when he first heard them—footsteps, hollow-sounding and echoing, as he would have directed them in a movie. He walked on as before, tossing his cigarette into a small puddle of water in the street and hearing it hiss minutely and angrily as it was extinguished. He wasn't too worried, for there was a marked absence of the hoodlum element here in the Executive Apartment area.

The man turned the corner half a block up and walked toward him. Walter felt a twinge of uneasiness. As the man passed one of the evenly spaced streetlights, Walter saw that he was well dressed, but like Walter his clothes seemed to have been hastily put on.

They closed in on each other, the hollow footfalls growing louder. Walter kept his eyes averted until he was a mere ten feet from the approaching figure; then he looked up and took in the man's appearance carefully—medium height, dark hair, a bit older than Walter's 35 and better-looking, wearing a half-buttoned light raincoat against the threat of showers. Walter braced himself and got ready for anything.

"Evening," the man said, smiling pleasantly. "Can't sleep either, huh?"

That was all. He didn't even break stride and was past Walter before he could think of a reply.

Walter let out his breath in relief. Sure! In a big group of buildings like this there probably were plenty of people who couldn't sleep, maybe even a few insomniacs in each building. And probably a lot of them walked at night just like Walter. It was a common thing, and so it was not so uncommon that they should meet occasionally in the early morning hours. Habit, as well as good sense, would tend to make them confine their pacing to the perfectly squared, well-lighted streets of the apartment area rather than stray out into one of the surrounding poorer neighborhoods. Walter didn't have a monopoly on insomnia.

Walter's deduction turned out to be right, for he happened to meet the same man the next night on East Street. This time Walter nodded pleasantly as they passed. Then the night came when the man asked Walter for a light, and they struck up a conversation and introduced each other.

The man's name was Alan Kirkland, and it turned out he lived three blocks from Walter in Executive 20. All the apartment buildings were numbered, from 1 through 60, and they all rented for the same exorbitant amount, with the exception of Executive 1, which rented for more. Prestige.

It turned out that this necessity for prestige had caused Kirkland, like Walter, to begin living at the very limit of his means. But now there were unexpected bills to pay, and Kirkland couldn't sleep.

It seemed to Walter, as their acquaintance progressed, that Kirkland was leading up to something. And one cool night when they ceased their aimless walking to sit on a hard bus-stop bench, Walter got an inkling of what that something was.

"Have you ever wondered, Walter," Kirkland asked as he leisurely packed his briar pipe, "how many insomniacs like you and me there are in a big project like this?"

"Often," Walter said.

"And as you know, Walter, lots of us, when we can't sleep, *really* can't sleep—we almost *have* to get outside and walk. You know, there are a lot of people out walking the streets in the early morning, more than most people think. You go stir crazy otherwise."

"Indeed you do," Walter said, watching Kirkland fire up the briar, noticing little flecks of gray shimmering in the dark hair on his temples.

Kirkland flicked the match away. "The fact is, Walter, a number of us early-morning insomniacs have gotten together to form a sort of club."

"Club?" Walter asked. "What do you do?"

"Why, we meet, Walter. Like all clubs, we meet."

"That's interesting," Walter said. "The Insomniacs Club."

Kirkland sat quietly puffing on his pipe, volunteering nothing more. It was just like him to catch the conversational ball and tuck it in his pocket.

"How, uh, many are there in your club?" Walter asked.

"Counting me," Kirkland said, "nine. Six men and three women."

Women, Walter thought with a sudden flush. He had a wild notion of what Kirkland was driving at. Too wild a notion of what Kirkland was driving at. Too wild a notion, he told himself, a little bit ashamed. He'd been faithful to Beulah for the eleven years of their marriage. Though from time to time he couldn't help asking himself why.

Kirkland swiveled his body on the bench to face Walter. "Have you considered," he asked in a confidential tone, "that there are certain advantages to friendships formed after midnight? Though we members of the club know one another, we know little *about* one another except for our common bond of insomnia. And more importantly, no one, none of the day people, connect us with one another—to them we are perfect strangers."

Walter swallowed. "You mentioned certain advantages?"

Kirkland smiled. "I named them, Walter, I named them. It's up to us to use them."

"But how?"

Kirkland placed a hand on Walter's shoulder, somehow making Walter feel uncomfortable. "Suppose you come along to our meeting tomorrow night?" Kirkland asked through teeth that clenched the pipestem. "It isn't anyone that we invite, you know. The membership is limited."

Walter considered asking why but thought better of it. He fought down his hesitance and for once decided to act on impulse. "I'm honored," he said, and then in an attempt at a joke added, "After all, I haven't much else to do."

Kirkland's hand tightened on his shoulder. "You'd be surprised, Walter." He smiled broadly around the pipe and stood up. "I'll meet you here tomorrow night—say at three?"

"Fine," Walter said, getting to his feet.

They parted, both men trying to beat the dawn home.

The next night Kirkland took Walter to the meeting in an apartment of a bachelor member of the club, a very fat man named Leon Stubbs. By 3:15 A.M. they were all there, sitting as comfortably as possible on Stubbs's modern furniture and sipping his liquor. Walter had been given a particularly strong martini.

"I suppose we should get the meeting under way," Kirkland said, standing and walking to a part of the room where he was visible to everyone. He seemed to be the unofficial president of the club. Walter glanced nervously around at the club members, whom he'd been introduced to and half of whose names he'd already forgotten. For a fleeting moment he wondered if he could be home in bed dreaming.

"Now," Kirkland went on, his voice like a pinch to Walter's idle thought, "we have a new candidate for membership in the person of Walter Thorn. I've known Walter fairly long and I've talked to him considerably of many personal matters. I think he's the man to make our final member."

Walter noticed that the members were paying rapt attention. The men, some of them with pajama cuffs showing beneath trousers or shirts, sat as if at a business meeting. The women wore the look that Beulah had when she was talking long distance to her sister in Washington. Walter had been disappointed to find that two of the women were quite average-looking, but the other, a Miss Morganford, was a somewhat more promising blonde. Miss Morganford, wearing dark slacks and bedroom slippers, was sitting next to Walter on the sofa.

"If you recommend him, Alan," Stubbs said, "I don't think we'll find much fault with him."

"That's right," a fortyish woman with horn-rimmed glasses said. "After all, it was Mr. Kirkland who brought us together."

Kirkland produced his briar pipe from a pocket and stood for a moment thoughtfully rolling it between thumb and forefinger. "I propose that we acquaint Walter with the purpose of our club and let him decide whether or not he wishes to join. Take my word that he's an honorable man, and if he chooses not to join us I'm sure he'll remain silent. Anyway, things should be got into operation as soon as possible. For some of us the need is quite pressing and further delay would be foolish."

Walter heard some of the members exhale loudly and a tall red-headed man shifted uncomfortably.

"Well?" Kirkland asked.

The members murmured assent.

Kirkland smiled and addressed himself to Walter. "The fact is, Walter, like all of us here you have an increasing need for money; you're bogged down, bored with your work, unhappy, not getting any younger. And if it isn't a need for money that's robbing you of your sleep, it's something that can be alleviated by money. Life has become nothing more than a monotonous struggle."

Walter bowed his head uneasily.

Miss Morganford touched his knee. "It doesn't hurt to admit it," she said in an understanding voice.

"All right," Walter said softly, "I admit it."

"So much I've learned from our conversations, Walter," Kirkland said more to the members than to Walter. "And I want you to know that you're among friends here."

Walter forced a smile. "Then the purpose of the club is sort of—group therapy?"

Leon Stubbs chuckled, but Kirkland pursed his lips thoughtfully.

"In a way," Kirkland said, "only we intend to do something specific about our common problem."

"But what?"

"Eliminate it." Now Kirkland lit the briar and puffed miniature clouds of smoke into the room. "As I said before, Walter, there are certain advantages to after-midnight friendships." He waved the pipe to take in all the occupants of the room. "We know one another, trust one another, but to the daytime world there is nothing to connect any of us." His eyes narrowed behind the smoke. "Here is a fact that can be used to our advantage." He focused his narrow eyes on Walter. "Tell me, does you wife know when you leave the apartment at night?"

"I've mentioned it sometimes," Walter said, "but usually she doesn't. She sleeps like a log."

"It's a curious fact," Kirkland said, "that the mates and family members of most insomniacs do sleep like logs. It reduces the risk of our plan to an absolute minimum."

"But just what is the plan?" Walter asked, noticing that the back of Miss Morganford's hand still rested against his leg.

Kirkland looked at him with a sardonic but respectful smile. "It's illegal—you should know that before we go further."

Walter put his hands on his knees as if to stand. "You'd better not go any further," he said nervously. "I don't want to be responsible for hurting anyone."

"Oh, wait," Miss Morganford said pleadingly. "At least hear us out. I'm sure you'll change your mind. I wouldn't hurt anyone either."

"No one will be hurt," Kirkland said reassuringly. "Only some big insurance companies, and for amounts that, while substantial to us, they'll hardly miss."

Walter sat back. "Then the crime is stealing."

Kirkland nodded.

"From who?"

"Why, from each other. That's why there's no risk; the victims will cooperate."

"I don't understand," Walter said as Stubbs poured him another ready-mix martini.

"Look," Kirkland said, brandishing the briar pipe, "suppose one of us here in this room burglarizes another's apartment at a set time when it's perfectly safe? Suppose every one of us here in this room burglarizes another's apartment? None of us are known to be acquainted. To the police it will simply look like ten unconnected crimes pulled off by the same thief, because we'll use the same *modus operandi* each time. They'll think a professional burglar is working this area."

"It makes sense," Walter said, sipping his drink. "And the insurance—"

"Exactly! Each of us has some heavily insured jewelry. When it's stolen we'll each collect the insurance money. I've arranged for the jewels to be sold to a reliable fence, and the proceeds will be evenly split among us." He grinned. "Pays better than an accountant's job, Walter, and it's just as safe—safer. Several insurance companies will be involved, so they'll pay off and will hardly bother to check. And you'll never have to worry about anyone here talking, because we'll all be equally guilty—and we'll all find it equally profitable."

Walter finished his drink slowly. "It *does* sound foolproof—"

"You think about it, Walter," Kirkland said, still smiling. "I'm sure we can rely on your silence in the meantime. Heck, I'll bet you wouldn't want Beulah even to know you were here."

"No," Walter said shakily, "I wouldn't. Yes, I will think about it."

The club members, in a noticeably more relaxed mood, lapsed into amiable chatter as another round of drinks was served by Stubbs, and before the sun came up, the meeting was adjourned.

Walter thought the matter over for a week. Each night while walking the streets he would just happen to run into Kirkland and his persuasiveness, and Miss Morganford even broke the rules of the club to telephone him and personally urge him to join. It was no wonder that at the next meeting of The Insomniacs Club, Walter became a member and was told the details of the plan.

He was shown how the lock on Stubbs's front door could easily be slipped with a piece of celluloid, and all Executive Apartment locks were of the same type. A piece of celluloid would be dropped at the scene of the first burglary to establish the method of entry, but from then on the doors would simply be left unlocked. On each robbery the same pair of ribbed gloves with a distinctive identifying mark on the forefinger would be used. The future burglars were all reminded to leave glove prints.

An irregular schedule covering five weeks was worked out, with the apartments of successive victims arranged in an unsymmetrical and unpredictable pattern. Walter's apartment was to be robbed last because he'd just increased his insurance and a five-week interval would be least suspicious. Each victim told the time of night or early morning most convenient for the crime to be safely committed and made sure his or her future burglar knew exactly where every member of the family slept and exactly where the jewels were kept. The victim was to mess things up a bit before retiring for the night, so the burglar could get in and out quietly and in a hurry.

As for the choice of burglar and victim, each member would be a burglar the crime before he himself would be victimized. Thus before any attention at all was cast on him he would have the previous crime's loot safely hidden away outside the apartment project. He would then leave the ribbed gloves in an agreed-on spot in *his* apartment for his burglar to slip on as soon as he wiped off the doorknob and entered. This way there was no chance of anyone being caught on the street before a burglary with the incriminating gloves, for they would be waiting conveniently at the scene of each crime.

And with the loot hidden in nine different spots—nine because it would be safer not to have the necessary first victim commit a later robbery—there would be no chance of anyone absconding with the jewels; so when they did sleep, the club members would rest easier. It would all be finished before the police had even a chance to get a whiff of anything suspicious. On a date a few weeks after the last burglary, The Insomniacs Club would meet again, the loot would be given to Kirkland and, on his insistence, two elected club members would go with him that morning to sell it and hold the money. At a meeting the next night the small fortune would be divided in equal shares.

Everyone made sure of his instructions, and until the future wave of jewel thefts that was to sweep over the Executive Apartments had ended, club meetings were postponed.

Things seemed to progress with incredible smoothness. Three days after the last club meeting Walter read on page 8 of the newspaper how $10,000 worth of jewelry had been stolen from Miss Mary Gordon, a resident of the Sterling Executive Apartments. Walter smiled to himself as he sat across the table from Beulah and read this item. He knew that a tall redheaded man named Fenwick had committed that robbery, and he knew that in two nights Miss Morganford would walk into Fenwick's apartment, slip on the same gloves, and relieve the Fenwicks of their jewelry. Then, four night later, it would be Miss Morganford's turn to be robbed. And eventually—here Walter did smile behind the paper—it would be his, Walter Thorn's, turn.

The plan seemed to be working so flawlessly that Walter actually looked forward to his turn with delicious anticipation. On September 11th at 2:15 A.M. he was to walk into Alan Kirkland's apartment, slip on the gloves he'd find under the entrance-hall throw rug, and walk to the door of the master bedroom—Walter knew where this was because his apartment was laid out the same way. Kirkland, who would already have displaced things in the apartment while his wife was sleeping, would be lying next to his soundly sleeping mate and actually watching as Walter walked to the top-left drawer of the triple dresser and quietly emptied Mrs. Kirkland's jewelry box. Then, a scant two minutes after he'd entered, Walter would make his exit, touching things here and there to leave the distinctive glove prints.

As Walter waited his turn, he watched the newspaper stories on the robberies move through editorials and lingerie advertisements toward the front page. And as more robberies occurred, police protection in the apartment project increased. This meant little or nothing, for the police were pathetically undermanned and the Executive Apartment area was large. Only once during a late night walk did Walter see a police car cruise by, and then it was two blocks away. Getting in and out of the apartment buildings unseen posed no problem. In fact, so helpless were the police that they had the newspapers explain the method of entry in the rash of jewel thefts and urged all citizens of the area to install special locks on their doors. And some citizens did—but not the citizens who counted.

As Walter knew it eventually would, the early morning of September 11th came to pass, and he found himself walking silently down East Street on his rubber soles toward Kirkland's apartment in Executive 20. The warm night was quiet and the street was empty, but still Walter felt an indefinable qualm, an unexpected queasiness at what he was about to do.

He shook this feeling off as he stepped down from the curb and crossed a deserted side street. He made himself think of how things would be after the burglary, picturing himself on Stubbs's sofa sitting next to Miss Morganford, each of them drinking a martini and counting their part of the proceeds.

Then he was in the deep shadow of Kirkland's apartment building. Glancing up and down the dark street to make sure he was unobserved, he breathed deeply and casually entered, as if he lived there. He walked swiftly up the marble stairs and down the soundproofed hall, and before he knew it he was standing trembling in the Kirklands' entrance hall, just inside the front door.

Walter reopened the front door a crack and wiped the knob clean of his own prints with a handkerchief, closed the door again, then got out his small penlight, and found and put on the gloves. He moved across the deep carpet into the Kirklands' living room.

Walter flashed the penlight beam about as he moved silently toward the master bedroom. Kirkland had done his job, opening drawers, tilting picture frames, overturning lamps. And he'd done it all with the telltale gloves, so even if by some wild quirk Walter was seen entering and leaving the building it would mean nothing, for the thief would have had to spend at least twenty minutes to search so thoroughly before finding the jewels. Walter would be gone in less than two minutes.

He entered the bedroom cautiously, seeing the two figures on the double bed. The drapes were partly open and there was enough light in the room to get the jewels without the aid of the penlight. Walter held his breath, moved to the correct open dresser drawer, and reached inside. His hand closed on the jewels in the open box and he began to stuff his pockets.

"What is it, dear?"

The woman's voice cut through Walter's body like a blade of ice.

"What the hell?" Kirkland's voice said.

There was a rustling movement on the bed behind Walter, then an ear-shattering scream, long and loud. A string of pearls broke in his clenched hand and the pearls went bouncing about the room. "Oh, good Lord," Walter moaned aloud, and he was out of the bedroom and running.

He hit the apartment door and fumbled it open, then he was dashing down the hall toward the stairs. There was light, and voices around him. A door opened down the hall and a small bald man stuck his head out, shutting the door partway and peering out curiously at Walter as he flew past, like a man watching a mad dog, ready to slam the door if it veered in his direction. Walter stumbled down the marble stairs, crashed into the front door, and was out in the street.

Windows were now lit up and sirens were wailing as he ran down East Street.

"Stop him!" Kirkland shouted—and that's when Walter knew.

It became clearer to him with every jarring step, with every stab of pain in his ribs. He'd been chosen to make the pattern complete. The robberies wouldn't be investigated further by the police because the thief would already have been apprehended. Naturally the thief would concoct some fantastic story rather than say where he'd sold the jewels and hidden or spent the money; so the insurance companies would take their losses and decide the jewelry had vanished in the mysterious channels of the underworld. And to prove Walter's guilt beyond question, after his arrest the robberies would stop.

A siren screamed unbelievably loud and a police car suddenly screeched to a rocky halt directly in front of Walter. He tried to spin on his heel but he tripped and fell sobbing on the suddenly bright pavement. He heard two more cars squeal to a stop and headlight beams blinded him.

Iron-strong hands yanked Walter to his feet and he was leaned against the rough brick wall of Executive 16 and expertly searched. They collected the evidence—the stolen jewelry and the ribbed gloves. He could hear them asking him at the station, "Where were you on this night and that night?" "I go out walking," he'd answer; "I have insomnia." He could hear them laughing.

His arm twisted behind him, he was led back up the street toward a waiting patrol wagon. He could feel hundreds of eyes on him as he lowered his head in defeat and shame. "Alan—" he pleaded to Kirkland as he was led past the crowd of onlookers, but it was natural that the thief would case his future jobs and know his victims' names. The shame cut deeper as he was pushed up into the back of the patrol wagon.

But to Walter the worst part of all was when the door of the patrol wagon was slammed shut. Then for the first time he was plagued by the vision of endless future nights—nights when he would wake up perspiring in a ten-by-ten cell, and there would be noplace to go.

by PHILIP WYLIE

NOT EASY TO KILL

Captain Ross, master of the transatlantic luxury liner Il-vania, was disturbed. He scented trouble—or worse. Twice since the Ilvania started back to the United States, the mul-timillionaire Emerson Stickney had nearly been killed.

Accidents? Attempts at murder? Everyone aboard was tense, apprehensive—as if the crew and all the passengers were feeling some sort of psychic expectation of disaster. . .

Meet an interesting cast of characters in this short novel, complete in this volume: the pompous Senator Prichard; mysterious biochemist, Dr. Moklokus; ambitious, scheming Senor Centora; Stickney's breathtakingly beautiful secretary, Marian Bates; and young Mark Adams, the ship's doctor, who finds himself in an incredible situation that compels him to combine detecting with doctoring. . .

Captain Ross, master of the *Ilvania*, walked along her boat deck through the warm and sluggish night. Smoke from the cherry-red tip of his cigar eddied behind him. Overhead, smoke also streamed from the two funnels of the passenger ship.

The Captain walked quietly, in a vague after-dinner mood. He was not thinking concretely but, rather, wondering and worrying. Presently he stopped.

Standing near one of the lifeboats was Dr. Adams, the ship's surgeon. A young man. He had taken off his hat. An aura of radiance from the deck below silhouetted his long nose, his sharp chin, his firm lips, the wind-stirred crest of his curly hair. The Captain had resented his youth when he had taken him aboard in New York. He had grumbled to the First Officer, "Doesn't even look like an intern."

But Dr. Adams had been polite, competent, and popular.

Popular. The Captain thought about that. Popular with the passengers. Popular in Paris with Miss Marian Bates.

She had fallen in love with him—and probably he had with her.

Ordinarily the Captain would not have considered it a concern of his. Young people fall in love. But Marian Bates was the private secretary of Emerson Stickney. Because she was infatuated with the *Ilvania*'s doctor, she had arranged that Stickney should return to America on that ship.

Perhaps Stickney had known. Perhaps not. Stickney was a rich and powerful man. His presence on the Ilvania had attracted other personages who wished to confer with him in the leisure of sea voyaging: Dr. Moklokus, who was president of the Stickney Research Foundation; Senator Prichard; Hypolito Centora, a South American millionaire.

Captain Ross would ordinarily have been glad to have Emerson Stickney aboard. Stickney held a controlling interest in the shipping company which owned the *Ilvania,* and Captain Ross had become his friend in the course of many crossings.

Indeed, years before, when Ross had been a Third Officer, Stickney had found beneath his silent and taciturn exterior a well-informed and imaginative mind. And, although no mention had ever been made of the fact, Ross had discovered himself master of a ship soon after. Thus, the voyage might have been felicitous.

But there had been trouble. A scent of trouble. It hung now in the heavy, heated night. It seemed to breathe a melancholy uncertainty into the music of the dance orchestra. It was really nothing—but it had infected all the passengers with an unnatural tenseness, a psychic expectation of disaster.

Captain Ross was a large and squarely made man. One would not have believed him attuned to inflections that had almost no existence. But he had spent his life on ships, at sea. He had developed a sixth sense. Or a seventh.

The doctor turned from the rail and stuffed tobacco into a short pipe. He saw the Captain.

"Good evening, sir."

"Evening, Doctor." The Captain slowly crossed the boat deck, and the two men stood together. The *Ilvania* slid a few hundred yards toward America, carrying its people and its music.

"About that leak," the Captain said finally.

"That's what was on my mind," the young man answered. "A coil in a refrigerator can break down—as that one did. It lets out a poisonous gas. And if a nearby ventilation tube has become disjointed through wear, it will carry the gas into whatever stateroom it serves."

There was a pause. "Stickney wasn't harmed?"

"Not a bit. A light sleeper, I presume. If it had been carbon monoxide, it would have killed him. Sulphur dioxide merely woke him up."

The Captain nodded. "It looked accidental."

"Exactly."

"I hadn't told you that Stickney was almost killed—again accidentally—when he came aboard?"

The doctor's face turned quickly toward the Captain. "No, sir. You hadn't."

"He was coming up the gangplank. There was a pile of trunks on A deck. One of them slid overboard."

"And barely missed him, eh?"

"I didn't see it happen. He glanced up, I'm told, as if he had heard it begin to slide. He dodged it. Nobody was seen near the trunks—they formed a regular labyrinth. And—again—one of them *could* have become unbalanced."

"I suppose men like Stickney have enemies."

The ship's master shrugged. "Their millions make them. . .Have you discussed the matter with Miss Bates?"

"Only casually. I—"

There was a silence. "You were going to say—?"

"I was going to say"—the younger man's voice took on a deliberately steadied quality—"that I'm afraid, Captain, I've fallen pretty thoroughly in love with that girl. I met her, as you may know, in Paris. I believe"—his confusion increased—"she persuaded Mr. Stickney to take the *Ilvania* on my account. You see, we are planning to get married— sometime soon."

The Captain said, "Hunh!" and smoked. Then he continued, "I wouldn't like to have anything happen to Stickney on board my ship. Maybe the trunk and the leaking gas were accidents. But I don't think so. When casual news makes the hair on the back of your neck creep—"

Dr. Adams nodded.

In a stateroom on A deck Marian Bates was standing in front of a mirror. She was singing softly to herself. A brunette with black eyes and white skin. Acquisitive, passionate, composed—a person of flickering inner thought, who looked both bold and secretive.

She was about twenty-two or -three. If Stickney had been less powerful and more quick to anger, if Miss Bates had been less poised, her position as his secretary might have caused comment. She was extravagantly beautiful.

There was a knock at her door. She said, "Come in," so melodiously that it was almost a part of her song.

The door opened. Emerson Stickney stood there, grinning. He was tall, broad, hard, tanned, grizzled. A man of fifty, with flashing eyes, beetling brows, and a jaw like a weapon. He wore a dinner jacket. His grin, which had been merry and faintly satanic, ebbed into boyishness.

"You don't need to decorate yourself for the doctor. Nature did better than all the dressmakers on earth could."

"Thanks."

He walked into the room. "Serious about him, aren't you?"

She looked at Stickney. The man of silent might. The man for whom Presidents sent. The man to whom the twanging accent of his native Maine still stuck.

"The doctor is mine—forever," the girl said.

His smile dropped. His brows knit. "Mean it, don't you?"

"I mean it."

"I hope you're right. I don't want to see a good secretary throw herself away. And you'll be quite a responsibility. Have you told him just how much of a responsibility?" His grin returned.

"No."

"How bad a disposition you have—?"

"No."

"Better do it. Or I will. I want to talk to him, anyway."

"You let me do all the talking."

Stickney laughed boyishly. "I would if you told the truth. But I saw you last night. Kissing, my dear, is not talking. All right. He looks good. His stock's old and sound—you can tell that from his face. He started at the bottom. So did I. If he's good enough for you, you'll get my blessing."

The girl walked up to Stickney, kissed him lightly on the forehead, and said, "I'd marry him in a minute without it, you know."

Dr. Adams and Marian Bates stood in the bow of the ship with their arms around each other. "I wouldn't want you to go on working for Stickney," he said. "But my salary is terribly small. You could have a little apartment, and three meals a day. Maybe one canary—and that's about all."

"It would be—plenty."

He kissed her; then he said, "I've been meaning to ask you—about your parents. I know your mother is dead—"

"I was born in Chicago," she replied, "and the less we say about my family the better. Mind?"

"No."

"What about yours?"

"Poor," he said. "I guess I've always wanted to be a doctor. It's not easy to work your way through college and medical school, but I was lucky. A couple of doctors and a couple of professors helped me. I wanted to do research. But when my internship ended—I had to eat. One of my faculty friends heard of this job. Someday we'll hang out a shingle and go into the real surgery business."

Marian touched his cheeks softly with her lips. "And we'll hope that rich people get in automobile accidents outside our door every day."

They laughed. They were in love. They were being sweet and gentle and kind to each other. Their words were full of desire. But in the dark over the ship hung the sword which the Captain had detected, and now the young doctor felt it.

"I meant to ask you. Did either you or Mr. Stickney ever think that the gas which leaked into his room the other night might have been no accident?"

"I don't think so. No."

"Did you know that a trunk fell overboard and nearly hit him as he came up the gangplank?"

"He mentioned it."

"I suppose a man like Stickney has hundreds of enemies."

"If he has," she answered, "it's because his enemies are crooks or cowards or thieves. He's a pretty swell person." She considered. "Of course, people have tried to kill him in the past. He isn't easy to kill."

"Not very comforting."

"I don't think there's anything in the idea." She observed that another couple were strolling along the deck, toward the bow. "Let's go and see how the bridge game is progressing."

In the smoking room Stickney was playing bridge. Stickney's partner was Dr. Moklokus. A huge, bald, pallid man with slate-colored eyes. They played against the booming-voiced Senator Prichard and sleek, gray-haired Senor Centora.

As Stickney's secretary and the doctor entered, they were settling their debts. Senor Centora and the Senator had taken out pens. "One thousand two hundred and ten, eh?" the Senator said cheerfully.

Dr. Adams flinched a little. The sum would have meant much to him.

Pens scratched.

Stickney looked gleefully at his companions. He winked at the pale Rumanian who headed his institute. "The doctor, here, knows psychology. And I know burglary. You gentlemen shouldn't have asked us to play." He turned. "Hello, Miss Bates, Doctor. How's the weather?"

"Hot," Marian answered, "and gloomy."

Stickney looked at his check and folded it. "We had a fine game."

"And a fine conversation," Dr. Moklokus added. "Emerson and I confounded our opponents throughout the game by talking about murder."

The eyes of the celebrated savant met those of the humbler member of his profession. "You're a doctor. You could have contributed. We four have been trying to decide the best method of killing a person without being detected. I suggested an overlong exposure to radiation. A needle in the medulla. Aconite. The Senator was more brutal, Senor Centora appallingly sadistic. And Emerson merely contented himself by telling of a few murders he's known of in the Orient."

The men had turned their chairs. Dr. Adams brought two more for Marian and himself. He had a feeling that in this conversation dwelt the essence of the Captain's intangible worries. Behind the macabre entertainment was—what?

Not murder.

A rich and politically important South American gentleman. A Senator. A world-famous doctor. Not murderers.

The young man smiled. "I'm afraid I haven't any ideas," he said. "Murder is the one thing I'd be scared to try."

"But supposing," Dr. Moklokus continued, "you had to murder someone? What method would you choose—if it were only a matter of that choice?"

Stickney leaned forward. "Exactly."

"Well—then—I'd get my victim alone—and kill him— and deny it afterward. Take him hunting and shoot him, and swear it was an accident."

He again looked at the three men who had been playing bridge with Stickney. "Or take him out on deck and push him overboard."

"This," Marian said suddenly, "is my idea of a dull conversation."

She rose, and as the others stood, Stickney touched the arm of the ship's doctor. "Like to see you in my stateroom."

Both men excused themselves. When they were out on deck Stickney said, "Wanted to talk to you. Here." He unlocked a door that opened directly from the deck.

His stateroom was large and impressive. Queens had occupied that stateroom—and princes—and gamblers.

Stickney drew up chairs beside a table. He said to the young doctor, "Sit."

Mark Adams, M.D., a bright young man with slim prospects. Emerson Stickney, for whom Presidents sent when there were crises in Central America.

"My secretary tells me that she wants to marry you."

Mark Adams nodded. "I want to marry her. I love her."

"She is an extraordinary girl. I'm very fond of her. She's been with me as my secretary for three years. She has brains."

"I know it. I don't deserve a girl like that. I have ambitions, naturally. I think I will do some decent surgery someday. And I have a few ideas I'd like to work out by clinical and laboratory investigation."

"Suppose I told Moklokus to give you a job?"

The young man shook his head. "It would be immensely generous of you. But I've made every inch of my way so far in this world, Mr. Stickney. And I couldn't take a job now from the employer of the girl I'm going to steal from him."

"Where'd you go to college?"

"Yale."

"Work your way through?"

"Yes."

"And through medical school?"

"Cornell."

"And now you want to marry this girl. To stow her in a little apartment in New York while you commute back and forth across the Atlantic in order to earn her a few cheap dresses a year and three meals a day she cooks for herself."

"It won't always be just that. But I intend to begin exactly like that—if she's willing."

Stickney grunted. "All right. I'm glad you're determined. You see, I'm pretty keen not to have Miss Bates marry a wrong guy. I like you. I like what you've done in your life so far. But to get and keep a girl with her spirit you'll have to accomplish more."

"I know it."

"All right. How would you like to do a favor for me?"

"I'd like to."

Stickney took a cigar from a humidor on the table. He lighted it attentively. "Mark," he said, producing with that word almost as much shock as he did with those that followed, "what do you think my chances are of getting off this boat alive?"

The doctor paused and returned the steady gaze. "Then

the trunk—the refrigerator leak—weren't accidental?"

"I think not."

"Who's doing it?"

Stickney shrugged. "I wish I knew. Who? A hired thug in the crew? A passenger? I don't know. A friend? Somebody is trying to kill me. They have been for the last two weeks I was in Europe. If I were killed now there would be the devil to pay. My holdings—my interest—they'd need a steady rein. And I'd want my murderer caught—because otherwise he—or she—might go on doing harm."

Mark Adams was breathing tensely and slowly. "I see. I'll stand by when I'm not on duty. I'll speak to the Captain and he'll set up a guard."

"It isn't just for the moment that I'm thinking, Mark. You can guard me now. But when I get off the ship—well, when and if it comes I want to have a strong, intelligent hand behind my estates. And I want my death avenged."

"I'm afraid I don't know enough about you, or your business, to help. And if you expect this sort of thing, I think it would be better to take steps to prevent it."

"Can't. Not my way of life. I can't go hiding around, and wearing bulletproof vests, and getting people to taste my food." Stickney chuckled. "Listen, Mark. All this may be wrong. We may catch some annoyed ex-employee of mine who has been sniping at me. I doubt it. What I want to do is to give you the funds, the power, and the authority to act for me if anything does happen. You don't know much about me—but Marian does. So I want you to have my power of attorney. To be my chief executor."

Mark sat still. He stared at Stickney.

"I'm not insane," the older man said.

"I wasn't thinking that."

"You were—but we'll let it pass. Snap judgments of men have got me my best assistants. I think you have what it takes. You've got nerve—surgeons have to have it. You're sensitive. They have to be. Yesterday I radioed for a report on your work at school and as an intern. Dr. Spelman Grant, at the Medical Center, said you were the best man they'd turned out in ten years. That's more than enough. Now, I'm asking you if you will take over my whole estate and distribute it as I arranged—in case I am killed. Will you?"

The young doctor waited for a full minute. Then he said, "If you want me to—and if you think I can do it."

"Good. Because, Mark, you'd have to anyway—if you married Marian."

"I'm afraid I don't follow that."

"She's my daughter."

Stickney sat back, smiling.

Mark Adams had lost his color. He rose like a man struck hard enough to render him nearly unconscious.

Marian came into the room.

"You haven't any right to monopolize him for so long," she said gaily.

Then she saw Mark's face. She knew he had been told. Her words were tender. "Come on outside with me, Mark."

They walked up to the boat deck.

"I didn't know," he said. "Or I wouldn't have dreamed—"

"Nobody knows." She took his arm. "I'll tell you what happened. Father married his secretary secretly long ago in South Africa. In the first month they quarreled and separated. I was born. Mother died. Father was so bitter that when he heard about me he had me put in a "good home" and brought up—and he forgot me and I never knew who I was until I was eighteen. The people who raised me weren't told who my father was, either.

"When I was eighteen he came to see me. I looked like my mother. I'd gone to public schools and taken a commercial course. He's a curious and devious man. He told me that he had been a friend of my father—and he offered me a job as a secretary in his office. I took it—and went to New York. I soon became his private secretary—and then, one day, he told me. He said his jealousy had made him do Mother a terrible wrong.

"He offered me the most glittering debut in social history—everything. But I was scared. I hadn't been trained for such things. And I'd grown to be pretty crazy about him. We had a swell time that day and that evening at dinner—and when I asked him if I couldn't go on being his anonymous daughter—and secretary—at least till I'd learned about his world—he was terribly happy."

The doctor drew a long, tremulous breath. "Strange," he said.

"Darling. You mustn't mind. Don't you see? When I fell in love with you, I thought—if he knew that I was Marian Stickney he'd be stiff and formal and never dare talk to me. Oh—darling"—she realized that her explanation had not removed him from a sort of glassy calm, a studied aloofness—"it can't matter, can it?"

"I don't know, Marian. I wanted to fight for you. To work for you. I've hated the doctors I knew who married rich women in order to ease their careers."

"Rich women are still women," she said quickly. "Flesh, blood, feelings, hopes, romantic desires." Her voice rose. "Oh, I know what you think. You think I've tricked you. It's cheap of you! You should be telling me that my contribution to—us—will just make you able to get your work done sooner and better. Think of it, Mark! You wanted to be a surgeon. All right. You can have your own hospital. You had ideas for research. All right. You can have the whole Foundation. I've been dreaming of what you'd do when I told you—"

"And I was dreaming," he answered miserably, "of a two-room apartment—"

"But—please understand!"

He shook his head. "I'm afraid I can't. It wasn't your fault. But don't you see? What you get in life without winning—only ruins you—"

Suddenly she was angry. "Ridiculous! Some kinds of idealism are stupid—and your kind is one."

She left him and he did not follow her.

Twenty minutes later Stickney came up to him, "Marian's in her room crying her eyes out. Well, Mark, I understand you. We've played you a sort of dirty trick. But I'm going to play a dirtier one."

"I don't mean to be unappreciative," Mark replied. "But don't you see? I wouldn't have a wife—I'd have a millionairess. I wouldn't have a practice—I'd have a job as a sort of super-banker and custodian of funds."

Stickney talked to him for an hour. Then he gave up. He said with abruptness, "All right, Adams. We'll leave Marian out. But remember your promise. You're going to take over for me if anything happens to me. I've already made arrangements. I've found a couple of lawyers aboard and deposited signed and sworn statements with the Captain."

He walked away through the dark.

For a long time Mark smoked. He thought with aching irony of the devastating situation. Marian's millions had literally yanked her from his arms. They had taken away the romance, the intimacy, the equality from their relationship, and left only a rich girl trying to buy the object of her infatuation.

Mark was too proud to consider it. He could only ache with disappointment. He decided he was entitled to go back on his agreement to help in the Stickney affairs. He had been tricked into his promise.

Smoke poured into the starless sky. The dance music had stopped long ago. It was late. Below, somewhere, the night watch was hosing a deck. The *Ilvania* moved forward steadily, ominously.

Mark started below, and realized he would not be able to sleep. He walked around A deck. Marian was sleeping on that deck. And her father. He continued round and round.

There was no one stirring in the shadowy passageways, no one standing at the rail. Only the night and the water.

When he came around the deck forward and started astern for perhaps the tenth time, he saw another person. A passenger, half the boat length away, with his back to the rail. Even at that distance he recognized Stickney.

Mark was on the point of going below to avoid accosting Stickney. But, as his pace slowed, the man at the other end of the promenade suddenly gave a sharp, agonized cry. He buckled backward. There was no one near him, but he acted as if he had been struck.

Mark saw as he rushed forward that Stickney lost his balance. He teetered on the rail and fell into the blackness.

Mark heard the splash. Then, with all his strength, he yelled, "Man overboard!" and charged up the companionway toward the bridge.

His appearance there started things.

A quartermaster grabbed the engine-room telegraph.

The ship dragged as the screws were reversed. Voices yelled commands through speaking tubes.

Dim figures ripped the canvas cover from a searchlight, and its white finger raced out on the obsidian water. Davits creaked. Oars clattered. Other men leaped into places in a lifeboat.

Light burst along the top deck and the decks below. Passengers began to appear. Wakened officers hurried among them. "No alarm. Man overboard. We're putting about and sending over boats."

"Who was it?"

"Stickney."

Stickney. The multimillionaire.

Stickney went overboard. He committed suicide.

But it wasn't suicide.

Mark discovered the rope. A rope taken from a lifeboat and made fast to a davit. A rope on which someone had slid down from the boat deck to a point just above A deck—a point over the head of Stickney as he stood with his back to the water.

The man hanging on that rope had given one quick blow and perhaps pulled the stunned Stickney backward by the collar.

That was how Mark reconstructed it for the Captain. "I couldn't see anything well. He cried out, sagged, fell back, and dropped into the water. A man hanging above him on that rope would have been screened thoroughly. Just his arm might have shown for a fraction of a second. At that distance I couldn't have seen the blow struck even if I had been looking for it."

The Captain was satisfied for the moment. A steward came for the doctor. Miss Bates had fainted.

Mark hurried to her cabin. He had a glimpse of the small boat out on the water in the radiance of the searchlight.

Marian lay on her bed, a stewardess at her side.

But as soon as the stewardess moved away and Mark bent over her, she opened her eyes. With them she signaled that he was to get the stewardess out of the room. He sent her on an errand.

Marian spoke quickly, but in spite of the pressure of her thoughts her first words were, "Poor Dad! He was a swell person! I didn't really believe such a thing could happen."

"Are you all right?"

"I am . . . Mark, did you see anything at all, or find anything?"

"Just a rope made fast on the boat deck and dangling over the ship's side. Somebody slid down it to a place above your father's head and struck him."

Grief and pain in her eyes were subdued by the necessity of active thought. "Did Father tell you he had turned his affairs over to you?"

"He said he had."

"Then let everybody go right on thinking I'm his secretary."

Mark looked at her doubtfully. "I think you'll have to establish your identity."

She raised her head and stared at him. "I can't! Everybody on the ship knows you have been making love to me. Plenty of people know you had a long talk with Father tonight. If I reveal that I'm his daughter, and since you were the only person near him when he was killed, everyone will conclude—"

"That I did it." Mark had not thought of that. He sat silently for a moment and then, as he heard the stewardess hurrying back, he said, "I'm sure you'll be all right now, Miss Bates."

Then he left.

A second lifeboat had been put overboard. More than half the passengers were crowded around the rail, watching the eerie search.

Mark stood for a moment, frantically thinking. This was no time to think of his refusal to marry Marian. She needed help. She might even be in the same danger that her father had been.

The Third Officer hurried through the crowd. "The Old Man wants to see you."

Captain Ross was sitting behind a desk in the reception room of his cabin. Reports were being brought to him from the bridge. Several people were in the room, including Senator Prichard and Senor Centora.

The Captain looked up gravely. "Adams, I've received a call by radio from Stickney's lawyers saying that Stickney informed them earlier this evening that you were to be put in full charge of his effects and that you had authority to act for him. Explain that."

Mark met the Captain's cold gaze steadily. "I can hardly explain it. I've know Stickney only since we left Bordeaux. I'm engaged to his secretary. He called me into his cabin and told me that he was conferring on me powers of attorney and other authority."

"Why?"

Mark kept his composure, although he realized that the Captain, the Senator, and the South American were listening incredulously. "He said that he expected he might be killed—and he wanted someone to take over his affairs and the pursuit of his murderer."

"Was he drunk?"

Senor Centora spoke softly. "Not in the least, Captain."

"He must have been insane then, Adams."

"I think not, sir."

The Captain spread out copies of several radiograms. He said quietly, "From these messages I gather that Stickney made you virtual dictator of his estate. It is unreasonable. If he expected foul play, and felt that he needed a competent person in whose hands to put his affairs, he could have availed himself of Senator Prichard here, or Senor Centora, who is an old friend, or Dr. Moklokus, who is familiar with his great philanthropies. Instead, he selected you, a doctor with no knowledge of business, a young man whom he had known only a few days. There must be some further reason."

Mark shook his head. "I can give none."

Senator Prichard, who had been breathing heavily as he listened, said to Mark, "It's unbelievable that he appointed you to such a position!" He thrust out his jowled face. "I would like to know, Doctor, how it happens that a few hours after you receive this fabulous appointment, Stickney was murdered and you were the only one who saw him go overboard! Wouldn't it have been possible for you to have killed Stickney and then given your cry for help afterward?"

The Captain broke in. "We can make no accusations of that sort, Senator, until we are convinced that Stickney's body has been lost."

The Senator turned around. "You said yourself, Captain, that it was almost hopeless to look for the body of an unconscious man in the sea."

"I said 'almost.' " He turned to Mark. "That will be all for the moment, Dr. Adams."

It was morning. The ship was under way again and, although Captain Ross had delayed until after dawn to search for Stickney, all efforts had failed.

Dr. Adams went to his table in the saloon and breakfast. The passengers at his table were silent. Ostentatiously silent. Mark caught them glancing covertly at him, and he realized that the incriminating circumstances surrounding him were already common gossip.

When he had finished his breakfast, the Captain again sent for him, and now he found the ship's chief officer closeted with Dr. Moklokus.

Mark observed instantly that the Captain's manner toward him had changed. At the same time he noticed that the magnified eyes of the bald doctor were regarding him with a strange attention.

The Captain said, "I'm sorry I was so rigorous this morning, Doctor. You see, Stickney's murder is a thing of world-wide consequence. His elevation of yourself in his affairs is of equal consequence. However"—he glanced toward the bald man—"when Dr. Moklokus heard the Senator's opinion about the matter he hurried up here. His stateroom is not far from Stickney's. He has just told me that he was lying in bed reading when he heard Stickney cry out. He rushed to his window in time to see Stickney's legs go over the rail.

"He heard you running down the deck, saw you stop at the place where Stickney had fallen, and as soon as you shouted, 'Man overboard!' he began to dress, realizing that you would be perfectly competent to handle the immediate situation."

This fortunate testimony filled Mark with a sense of immeasurable relief. "That is certainly lucky for me! And I'm immensely obliged to you, Dr. Moklokus."

"Think nothing of it, my boy. As a matter of fact, now that I think of it, I heard you tramping round and round the deck, and in one of your absences I heard Stickney's door open. He couldn't have been standing by that rail for more than two minutes before he was struck. Whoever let that rope down must have expected him to take a late breather. I wonder if it was a habit."

"I couldn't say," Mark answered, "but perhaps Miss Bates could."

The Captain sent for Marian, who told them that Stickney often slept very short hours and that he had taken a post by the rail of the *Ilvania* on previous nights.

They discussed the situation at length. Captain Ross finally said to Mark, "It is, conceivably, the work of a stowaway. We will have the ship searched. I, myself, will cross-question all the persons aboard who knew Stickney or who talked to him on this voyage. I would like Miss Bates to go through all classes of the ship's passengers to see if she recognizes any persons who have had dealings with Stickney."

He looked at Mark. "Have you any further ideas, Dr. Adams?"

"Not at the moment, Captain. I'd like to go over the whole thing with Miss Bates."

"Certainly. As far as your authority to act in Stickney's stead is concerned I shall uphold it on shipboard. Mr. Stickney brought to me his sealed deputization of power yesterday evening. I opened those papers after my first conference with you this morning. Frankly, I can't see why Emerson Stickney chose you, but he did, and I respect his choice."

Mark shook his head perplexedly, and said, "If you'll excuse Miss Bates and myself—"

As soon as he had piloted her to a space out of earshot, he said. "It was swell of you to hold back the truth about yourself, because they suspected me of killing your father. But you don't have to do it any longer. Dr. Moklokus has cleared me." Rapidly he explained what had happened.

Marian took his arm, and then let go of it. "I don't think I want anyone to know about me yet," she said. "Look, Mark! If the world suddenly found out that I was his daughter, I might be killed the same way, mightn't I?"

"I don't know."

"As his daughter I would be thrown into a whirlwind. As his secretary I will be safe, and I can help you."

"Help me?"

At that precise moment a boy with a radiogram in his hand spied the doctor and delivered the message.

Mark tore it open and read:

DOCTOR MARK ADAMS
STEAMSHIP ILVANIA
WILL CHECK YOUR CREDENTIALS ON ARRIVAL STOP MEANWHILE ARE ACCEPTING YOUR AUTHORITY STOP HAVE YOU ANY INSTRUCTIONS STOP SUGGEST BUYING STICKNEY STOCKS WHEN MARKET OPENS AS NEWS OF MURDER WILL DOUBTLESS CAUSE DANGEROUS PRICE DROP STOP DO YOU AGREE STOP RADIO OR PHONE AT ONCE.

CYRUS BRADLEY
GORDON VANCE
MILTON G. DRESSER
L. Q. BLACK

Mark recognized some of the names. Black was president of the largest bank in the country. Vance was a utilities magnate. Bradley was a famous corporation lawyer. And they were waiting for *his* instructions!

His expression was so shocked that Marian took the message and read it.

She smiled at him. She almost laughed. "When I said 'help you,' Mark, that's what I meant. Father wanted you to take over his affairs if anything happened to him, because he thought you were going to be my husband and you'd have to manage them someday."

He turned a haggard face toward her as she continued, "Maybe you don't want a wife, but you certainly do need a secretary. I think we ought to radio back and tell them to buy just enough to prevent any dangerous sag."

"I guess so," he said hollowly.

Marian thought for a moment. "Radio them to use the funds in the Conover National Bank. I think there's about seven millions on deposit. It may not hold the market, but we don't want to pay any more interest on brokers' loans than we have to."

Mark, still more baffled by the mention of the sum of money which he was going to authorize spending, suddenly grinned. "You'd better write the radiogram, and I'll sign it. I guess I do need—a secretary."

His grin worked a sudden miracle in him. The diseased night had passed. Emerson Stickney had died. Marian had moved unutterably beyond his possession. But she was still with him, and would be for some time.

That brought him an abrupt and dazzling feeling of comfort. He held he did not know how much power, over he did not know what incalculable resources. His morbidly low spirits lifted.

He looked at the girl, still grinning. "Come on," he said. "The radiogram first. Then I want to talk to you."

They sent the radio message, then they went to the room that had been Stickney's.

Marian sat down, sensing the change in him. Mark walked slowly back and forth in front of her.

"Now," he began, "in the first place I haven't the faintest concept of your father's affairs. Have you?"

"I know a lot about them."

"Enough to make sense in managing them?"

"With the advice of the men he trusted—yes. Even without it—as long as we don't start anything."

"Start anything?"

"You know," the girl replied. "Buy a railroad or build a hydroelectric plant or promote a new project. As long as we just coast."

"Oh. All right. We'll coast. We'll wait until his will is

probated before we do more."

"Will they probate the will—without the body?"

"Certainly. It happened once while I was an intern. The body was destroyed, never found. Fire. But there was no doubt, no reasonable doubt, that the woman had been burned. So her will was probated and her estate divided."

"Then, sooner or later, I'll have to become known for what I am."

"Yes." He walked one length of the room. "We get in day after tomorrow. There'll be time enough then to consider that problem. The one thing to think about now is who killed him. Have you any ideas?"

"No definite ones."

"Meaning what?"

She shrugged. "What about clues?"

"There aren't any clues, except the rope. That's been put away for examination by experts."

"Father must have been struck with something."

"Probably thrown into the sea."

"There weren't any fingerprints or anything up on the boat deck where the rope was tied?"

He smiled. "Nothing we could see . . . Next point: Moklokus, Prichard, Centora. Do you know them well?"

"I know the doctor very well. He visited Father a good deal. You see, Father has put millions into the institute that Dr. Moklokus presides over."

Mark nodded. "And a fine institute, too. Doing some of the best biochemical research on earth. You think the Rumanian genius is okay?"

"Except for his looks."

"A lot of doctors are funny-looking . . . How about Prichard?"

"I don't think Father cared much for him. He's from a state in which Father owns two hundred and fifty thousand acres and employs about thirty-five thousand men."

"Gosh!"

She ignored his surprise. "He's a windbag. A demagogue. He curries favor with Father because Father is powerful in his political territory."

"Right . . . Centora, then."

"I never saw him before. He is from Belgian Guiana in South America. Father discovered gold there when he was nineteen. That was the beginning of his fortune. He built and owns the railroads. He owns a steamship company that trades there. The natives have a Spanish nickname for him that's translated into 'The Blue-Eyed Papa.' Centora is a rich *politico*. He's on the side politically that's against outside ownership. But cautious. It wouldn't do to cross Father publicly in Belgian Guiana."

"And all those three gentlemen happened to be in Europe and decided it would be useful to travel on the same boat with your father. Why?"

"Dr. Moklokus was attending a medical conference in Vienna. The Senator was on some mission in Germany. Centora was amusing himself in Paris. At least, that's what they say. But as to why they wanted to see Father . . . There are three good reasons. Father refused to renew Dr. Moklokus' contract as president of the Foundation, just before we went abroad."

Mark whistled. "Why?"

"The books weren't straight. Father called the doctor on the carpet and they had a furious argument."

"And Senator Prichard's reason?"

Marian drummed with her fingers on the arm of her chair. "I don't know much about that. Father hated crookedness. He made his money by imagination and energy. Exploitation, if you will. But never by treachery. The Senator, I just guess, was using knowledge of what the government would do, which he obtained in committees, for swelling his own purse. Father wrote him guardedly about it. I took the letter. And the Senator, after that, was very anxious to explain."

"What would your father have done?"

"Seen to it that he resigned—ill health. Or exposed him."

"That leaves Centora."

"Mr. Centora would like—like, I say—to be the dictator of Belgian Guiana. It's a republic under nominal foreign supervision. It will be—or would be—as long as Father stood in the way."

The young doctor sat down abruptly. "Three men whose

careers depended on your father, and whose careers were being threatened by your father, are on this ship. And those three gentlemen, only last night, were all discussing the best way to commit murder."

"And you suggested getting a man alone and throwing him overboard."

Mark looked at Marian.

Her eyes were steady.

He shook his head. Then he got up.

"What are you going to do?"

"Interview your father's friends."

She regarded him for a moment. "It's not a good idea."

"I think it is."

"All right."

He went toward the door. He turned. He was on the verge of saying something tender and personal.

She looked receptive. She said, "What?"

"Nothing. See you later."

He did not get to his interviews at once. His duties as ship's surgeon occupied him until bouillon was being served on the decks.

He found Senor Centora sprawled in a deck chair. The South American rose when Mark stood before him. "Ah, Doctor! I've wanted to congratulate you, since I heard you have acceded to the charge of the great Stickney's enterprises."

"Thanks. I wanted to see you."

Centora's smile was radiant. "I am honored," he said.

Mark leaned back in his deck chair. "I wanted you to acquaint me with the principal facts of the Stickney holdings in Belgian Guiana."

The South American smiled more broadly. "I shall be happy! Stickney made my country. He is our national hero. We have quarreled with him often—hated him never."

"You were quarreling with him on the voyage," Mark said, as if the fact were positive knowledge.

Centora's voice became minutely less pleasant. "A small quarrel. We wish to make slight changes in our government."

Mark took a shot in the dark. "And you proposed that Stickney cut in with you on handing over a dictatorship to you. You offered to drop out the other foreign property holders. What?"

Senor Centora politely accepted his broth from the deck steward. His smile, when the man had gone, was no longer in existence. He said icily, "May I be privileged, Dr. Adams, since you have so much power and wish foolishly to wave it in my face, to ask what your attitude from now on will be?"

Mark rose and stretched. "Can you climb ropes, Centora?" he asked.

Senator Prichard was amidships, talking to whoever would listen. He saw the doctor walking toward the group.

"Doctor!" he shouted. "I want a minute alone with you, old man."

"Fine. How about my dispensary?"

"Excellent."

The Senator sat down on a porcelain-finished chair and beamed. "I have a thousand pardons to beg of you, old man, for being so rude in the Captain's office this morning! I jumped to an idiotic conclusion when I insinuated that you might by any conceivable circumstance—"

"I might easily have done it," Mark answered calmly. "But I didn't."

The Senator lost a little of his enthusiasm for apology. "Of course not. A moment of calm reflection—"

Mark lit a cigarette. "Did *you* kill him?"

The eyes under florid folds of flesh, generally full of professional merriment, snapped briefly with a baleful and revealing shrewdness. "I get it, Adams. You have a right to accuse me. Tit for tat, eh? And pretty smart. If I'd done it, you'd have caught me thoroughly off my guard."

He laughed uproariously. "No, sir. Emerson was one of my most esteemed friends. And, by the way, I want to count you as a friend of mine, too. Emerson picked you to look after his estate, and, by George, I'm beginning to see what a clever fellow he picked!"

Mark said, "*M*-m-m-m. One clever fellow can discern

another, eh?"

Again the sharp flash of the porcine eyes. Again the humorous wag of the head. "Not guilty, Adams! I'm just a bull-headed politician. Started out as a cowhand in the old days. I—"

A bell rang. Mark answered a phone.

"Tell him I'll be right down." He looked at his guest. "Sick girl in the second class. I'll be seeing you, Senator. But if you were a cowhand, you must be very clever with ropes—as well as with anticipating Federal business moves, from your inside position."

The Senator tried to hide alarm by boiling to his feet. But Mark had opened the door. "Clever with ropes," he repeated, and left the apoplectic Senator.

Mark knocked on a door in a passageway. A cultured voice said, "Come in!"

Mark walked into the room. He smiled. "Doctor Moklokus."

The celebrated biochemist waved Mark into a chair. "Considerate of you to pay me this visit."

"I was just talking with the Senator."

"Ah?"

"A friendly person. Great men," Mark continued disarmingly, "are always simple."

A faint smile moved the pale lips on Moklokus' still paler face. "Almost always. A few are complicated. I, for example. Tell me. Why did Stickney suddenly authorize you to represent him?"

"Caprice. Whim."

"I've been wondering. Perhaps he was deeply in love with that girl. Perhaps when he found you had won her, he determined to leave her and her lover—yourself—possessed of his goods. Men in love have done stranger things."

Mark looked astounded. "I never thought of such a thing!"

"Then, too, he may have committed suicide last night. And left the evidences of an untraceable murder to keep his memory clear of the taint of self-destruction . . . I wanted," the bald man continued, "to speak of one or two things. As you know, my whole life is bound up with my work at the Foundation."

"I've always admired it."

Moklokus smiled. "Thank you. Now, Stickney refused, two months ago, to renew my contract."

Mark appeared surprised. "But why?"

The Rumanian pondered a moment. Then he said, in his low, eloquent voice, "In all men there are weaknesses. I am a strong man, Adams. Very strong. But I have had, since my days of abject poverty in Bucharest, an almost ungovernable lust for the possession of money. As president of the Foundation I handled staggering sums. And, about a year ago, acting in a trancelike manner—a hypnotic state, the product of long psychic accumulation—I embezzled about fifty thousand dollars from the Foundation."

Moklokus' face was impassive. "Stickney, of course, discovered it. I paid back the money at once. But he naturally refused to renew my contract. He had a fanatical hatred of dishonesty. I went to Vienna when he sailed this spring. I hoped to see him. I pleaded with him. He was adamant." Moklokus stopped there.

Mark looked at him for a long time. "Why are you telling this to me?"

The Rumanian spread his white, thick-fingered hands. "Because you should know. It will be you, now, who disposes of Stickney's estate—and of me, so to speak. I hoped that you, being a surgeon, might understand the values involved more completely."

His smile returned, slight now, and self-deprecatory. "Obviously, I would never again commit that crime. A treasurer could be set to guard me. But my work—is individual, and important."

Mark thought fast and hard. This was, evidently, the truth. Moklokus had intelligence enough to tell the truth—or part of it—to gain subtler ends. He rose and said, "Dr. Moklokus, if my influence is accepted, you may be sure that I shall keep your—lapse—a secret. And I shall use every energy I possess to have your contract renewed." He held out his hand.

Moklokus took it, impassively shook it, then turned his

head away. Mark left the room.

Mark ate lunch in abstraction, automatically responding to the congratulations of the passengers at his table. He spent two hours after lunch in the ship's hospital—thinking. Once or twice he walked out and through the ship. He saw Moklokus playing chess with Centora. Later he saw the South American talking with the Senator.

He spent a considerable period with the ship's master and his officers. Captain Ross had made as complete an inquiry as he could. But all his efforts added nothing to the known facts of Stickney's death.

At four o'clock Marian telephoned Mark.

He went to see her immediately, and told her in detail what had happened.

When he had finished, her eyes were glowing. "You're brilliant, Mark. Which one do you give first place to?"

"First place? They were all angry enough at your father to have killed him."

"What are you going to do next?"

"Wait and see what they say to me—after they have had time to fix up phony answers."

"Moklokus won't say any more."

"No." Mark suddenly started. "Marian! By golly! Think of this: perhaps Moklokus was asleep when your father was killed and never did hear or see anything. But when he learned I'd been given authority to act for the estate he went up and alibied me—to win my friendship."

"Or—" Marian said breathlessly.

"Or perhaps he wanted to alibi himself. When he got me out of a hole by saying he'd seen the entire thing, he naturally made all of us assume that he was tucked in bed. He may have seen me, all right, but from that rope."

Marian nodded slowly, several times. "That's a thought to be filed for later reference . . . Now. I've had the radiograms for you sent to me."

"What radiograms?"

She smiled. "The stock market's open. You should be standing at a ticker right now, with a phone in your hand. The Stickney holdings dropped—ten points. They then rallied a bit. The tickers carried the news that you were to represent Dad. That knocked off another five points. I radioed Black to announce secretly, but so it would get around the Street, that you had been in training for years as Dad's bright young man, and had been in virtual management of his properties for the last eighteen months. The rumor spread. The stock rose. We bought our own stuff, and are still buying, and will be for another twenty minutes."

Mark sat down on a chair. "So I'm a sensation in Wall Street."

"You're headlines—all over America."

"Gosh! Say, what are our holdings?"

Marian brushed back her dark hair with her hand. "Do you want to know? Well, Alaska Promontory, Cape Metals, Bicolor Pictures, Trans-America Gas and Light—"

"Never mind," Mark said. "I'm sorry I asked. Will you write them down? And a note about each?"

She nodded. "I was going to—before I called. But last night or this morning somebody came in and stole the typewriter from Dad's room. It was a portable. I've sent a steward to send up another."

"Anything else stolen?"

"No. The typewriter was on the desk, in its case—a black case—ready to be taken."

"Good," Mark answered absently. "I'll never learn all those securities. Never."

"You've got to," she replied. "I'll get it ready right after dinner. And you can cram. The whole world will meet you at the boat, and you've got to be able to seem glib. You'd better go now."

She smiled at him, and her smile made him stand unwillingly at the door.

Marian understood his expression. "Rich women have feelings," she said gently. "But you imposed the conditions, Doctor."

At midnight he threw himself, half dressed, on his bunk. He unfolded the long list of Stickney properties Marian had compiled. "AIP—Alaska Promontory. Gold mines. Valued at $2,250,000; 500,000 shares of common stock. Stickney owns 100,000. BGG—Belgian Guiana Gold. Common and Preferred—"

He realized that he was exhausted. He shut his eyes . . .

The *Ilvania* plowed toward America. And Mark slept. He slept while a million Americans spoke his name to a million others. Then it was heard for the first time in India and Australia and England in the hours of dawn. Around the world.

A knock on his door, soft but imperative, woke him. He sat up. "Yes?"

The white face of a steward peered in. "Doctor! Come at once."

"Somebody sick?"

"I think so, yes."

He pulled on his coat and snatched the black bag from a rack. He followed the steward.

Outside a first-class cabin stood two men—seamen—on guard. Mark saw the Captain coming down the passageway.

He stepped back.

Captain Ross jerked his head and went into the cabin first. Mark followed.

There was no one in the room. No one alive. The lights were all on. In his bed lay Senator Prichard. There was a revolver in his partly clenched hand. A .45.

A bullet had made a hole in his forehead and shattered the back of his skull. The pillow was drenched with blood.

Captain Ross shut the door of the cabin and said, "Shot was heard and reported by a passenger about ten minutes ago."

Mark bent over and stared at the butt of the revolver. He saw the initials *M.J.P.* engraved there.

"Killed himself," Mark murmured.

The Captain's face was grave and perplexed. "I don't understand it."

Mark's eyes had fastened themselves on the writing desk. He walked over to it. On it was a portable typewriter. He noted almost automatically that the case top lying beside it was blue—it couldn't be the one that had been stolen from Marian.

There was a sheet of paper in the machine. Several lines had been written on the paper. They were unevenly and rather clumsily typed.

What Mark read aloud was a message from Prichard: "It's no use. I killed Stickney. My reasons for doing it are private and will never be known."

"He was drunk when he wrote that," the Captain said.

Mark nodded. "He probably had something pretty serious on his mind. Prichard wasn't the sort of fellow who would take his own life without plenty of cause."

"No," Ross answered absently.

"There is nothing we can do here, anyway—"

Together they left the room. The ship's master instructed the men on guard to remain at their posts, and walked on deck with the doctor. Sometime later Mark bade the Captain good night and went to his quarters. He undressed slowly.

Stickney had been killed by Prichard. That was that.

He stretched out in his bunk with his eyes closed. The heavy night and the incubus which swam in it made his sleep uneasy. And he sat up tensely when there was another sharp knock on his door.

"Come in!"

It was a member of the crew to tell him that the Captain wanted him.

Daylight was streaming into his room. He glanced at his clock. Half-past eight. A few minutes later he presented himself at the Captain's cabin.

Ross nodded, and unrolled a pair of trousers on the desk top. "These were in Prichard's closet."

Mark picked them up. Except for the fact that they were crumpled from having been rolled, he noticed nothing unusual about them. They were a reddish-brown, heavy tweed. He remembered having seen Prichard in the suit.

"Take a good look at the outside of the right leg."

Mark repeated his examination, and then saw several small spots. "Blood?"

"That's what I want you to tell me," the Captain answered. "These trousers were hanging in Prichard's closet.

I went back to have another look at his things myself. I noticed those spots. He didn't dress for dinner on the night Stickney was killed, and he was wearing that suit. Now, if he had slid down the rope and hit Stickney, a few flecks of blood might have spotted his trousers. But there is a more significant item. Sticking to the insides of the trouser legs I found a couple of short hemp fibers."

Mark shook his head. "I'll take a look at those stains under the microscope. It'll be easy enough to tell whether they are human blood or not."

Half an hour later, Mark returned from the ship's hospital and made his report. "It was blood all right. That's a terrible thing to think of—Prichard sliding down that rope, slugging Stickney, and pushing him into the sea."

Ross looked searchingly at the doctor. "It is. Well—thanks, Doctor."

Mark returned to his quarters, bathed, shaved, and breakfasted. Then he went out on deck. The passengers were obviously depressed. Few people were sitting in the sunlight. Marian, however, was in her deck chair. He sat down beside her.

"Do you think," she said, "that Prichard killed my father?"

He nodded.

"I don't."

He turned quickly toward her. "We found bloodstains on the trouser leg of the suit he was wearing that night. And two or three hemp fibers—from the rope."

The girl was staring out to sea and talking in a low tone. "I could see Moklokus murdering somebody. Or Centora. He has ambition. But not Prichard, somehow. He was crooked. He was vain, and he wouldn't have liked the exposure of his little racket. But he's not a murderer."

Mark smiled. "A woman's intuition? You're upset."

"I'm not. And even if he were a murderer, he simply wouldn't commit suicide. He liked life too much."

"But the facts . . ."

"What facts?" Marian gazed steadily at Mark. "He was found dead with his own gun in his hand. All right. Somebody could have stolen his gun, shot him, and put the gun in his hand. It would take quite a while after the shot for anybody to get there. In fact, it did take quite a while. I asked. In that time a murderer could have easily gotten away.

Mark looked at the girl apprehensively. "But, Marian, that's not all—"

"Of course it's not all. But it would have been a cinch to steal those trousers and put blood and pieces of hemp on them. And that note was written on a typewriter. It wasn't in Prichard's handwriting. Anybody could have done that, too. Senor Centora spent the whole evening in Prichard's cabin. They were both drinking. Centora could have written that note by just pretending he was fooling with the typewriter—then shot Prichard or typed the note right after the murder."

"Wouldn't it be easier, Marian, just to assume that what very evidently took place *took* place? Wouldn't it be easier not to make up such elaborate explanations?"

She caught his arm. "Do you *really* believe Prichard committed suicide?"

"No."

She relaxed. "I didn't think you did."

"I don't believe it," Mark said slowly. "And I have a hunch Captain Ross doesn't believe it, either. But what can we do?"

"Nothing now, but I think that when Senor Centora gets off the boat tomorrow we ought to have detectives shadow him. I can arrange it by code right now."

Mark started to his feet. "That's a good idea. And what about taking the same precaution with Dr. Moklokus?"

"You were speaking of me?"

Mark turned his head and smiled blandly. Dr. Moklokus had emerged from a companionway in time to overhear the mention of his name. "Why, yes, Doctor. I was just telling Miss Bates about some of your work in histology."

The bald Rumanian nodded politely and moved down the deck. Mark turned to look back at him. Moklokus had also turned. The friendly expression which he had worn as he emerged from the companionway had vanished.

Five times during the afternoon Mark talked on the radiophone with New York, prompted by Marian. The men with whom he talked were men whose names he had seen in newspaper headlines. Mark gave the intricate operations which he conducted a calculated aspect of certainty and confidence.

He had to rely on his own invention often. Gordon Vance wanted to know if Stickney's philanthropies could count on their regular annual appropriations. Mark said they could. Vance also said that Moklokus' contract had come up for renewal. Mark ordered it renewed.

Black gave a statement of their market position. Mark requested that unless there was a further sag in the Stickney holdings, stocks be allowed to seek their own levels. Black called again to say that several large accounts were being quietly withdrawn from his bank. Mark put his hand across the telephone and reported that to Marian.

She said quickly, "We've got to do something to restore confidence there."

Mark, reducing the situation to simple elements because he could understand it no other way, whispered quickly, "Why don't we tell Black to buy another bank? Or to announce that he is negotiating to buy one?"

"Good! Suggest it," Marian said.

Mark did so.

Black's dignified voice took on a quality of excitement. "I'd thought of that, Dr. Adams, but I was afraid to offer it. May I say that in my opinion Emerson appointed a brilliant successor?"

Mark replied, "Thank you, Mr. Black," hung up, and grinned at Marian. "I make a first-rate tycoon."

Evening.

There was no festive dinner. No Captain's Ball. Conversations everywhere were subdued.

After dinner Marian and Mark sat together, until she said, "I'm going to try to get some rest. You'd better, too, because tomorrow you will find out what it means to be a national figure. And I suggest that you study your lessons in Stickney stocks."

176

Reluctantly he bade her good night.

He was very weary. He went to his cabin and pored over the stock lists. After two hours he went to bed.

The *Ilvania* steamed westward. Montauk Light had been sighted. In the hours after midnight the engines cut their speed and the ship moved into the harbor. She dropped anchor off quarantine. A police boat came alongside. But the murderer of Stickney had killed himself, and the work of the police would be only routine.

Just before daybreak the quarantine ship came out, loaded with reporters.

They woke Dr. Adams. They bribed a stewardess to waken Miss Bates. And, as the sun rose over the city, first Adams, then the girl, and later other passengers were interviewed and cross-questioned and photographed.

Mark had one brief moment of comparative privacy with Marian. They were standing on the boat deck. His face was taut and alert. "You stick with me everywhere I go today. Remember, you're my secretary."

She nodded, and smiled a little. "I remember offering myself for the position. You never really accepted me."

Mark grinned. "It's a fine position."

At lunch, downtown, with President Black of the Conover National Bank, with Vance, the utilities man, and Bradley, the corporation lawyer, Mark looked at Marian. His head spun. All the morning he had been with these celebrated men. He had been talking in millions and tens of millions. Of the situation in Washington. And of the provisions in Stickney's will. He was putting on a good act, but this was not his way of life.

In the afternoon he occupied Stickney's private office on the sixty-eighth floor of a skyscraper. He sat behind Stickney's desk. Marian was at his side. Men with great names came and went. On Mark's desk was a newspaper. Its front page carried his photograph, with the caption, *Czar of Stickney Fortune.*

Between his tightly packed and awesome appointments, Marian had time to say only such little things as, "You're doing fine!" and he to reply, "It's like playing God—"

177

Dinner with three men who had hurried up from Washington. Afterward he went to a suite which Marian had engaged for him at a hotel. At ten o'clock he was closeted with a railroad president who had flown from Chicago. At eleven he had time once again to talk with the reporters.

He found himself mouthing phrases that he had read as the words of other industrialists: "America cannot falter, because, if she wishes, she can be abundantly self-sufficient"; "Science and invention are the parents of wealth and employment—not its enemies."

Then it was one o'clock, and he found himself sitting in the reception room of his suite, looking with a sort of exhausted triumph at Marian.

"I guess," she said, "that's all for today."

"Except that I promised to write a couple of letters. If you've got the strength left, could you write them tonight?"

She nodded, and then hesitated. She picked up the telephone and asked for the desk. She turned to him before she spoke. "I've got to get a typewriter sent up. I forgot that mine was stolen."

She made her request and hung up. When she faced Mark again, she jumped to her feet. "What's the matter?"

Mark was pale. "You mean your typewriter disappeared just before your father died?"

"I guess so."

"It had been in its case on the desk that evening?"

"Certainly. Somebody stole it either before or after father was killed."

Mark's eyes were shining. "That's it! That means Prichard was murdered!"

Marian was frightened. "Mark! For heaven's sake—!"

"It must have been Centora! He was with Prichard that night, getting him drunk—"

"If you would just take it easy, Mark, and explain—"

"No time! What was the name of the detective agency that we cabled to watch Centora?"

Marian told him.

A moment later he was on the telephone. A man who spoke with painstaking slowness said, "Mr. Centora registered at the Colonnade Hotel, had dinner there, went to bed, and left a call for nine o'clock tomorrow morning. Then he got up, dressed, came down the stairway, and sneaked out of the lobby. He took a cab to the Stickney Foundation."

"When was that?"

"Twenty minutes ago."

Mark looked at Marian. "We're going to visit Dr. Moklokus at once. Come on!"

The Stickney Foundation was an enormous red-brick building on the edge of the Hudson River. Here and there lights burned on its impressive facade.

A doorman stopped them. Mark produced his card. "Dr. Stevenson sent for me. A friend of mine."

"Seventh floor. Laboratory K."

They took an elevator.

They got off at seven and walked through gloomy corridors. "What floor is Moklokus on?" he whispered.

"Third."

"We'll go down the stairs."

The door to the great scientist's private suite and laboratories was locked. They tiptoed into the room next to it and tried a connecting door. It was locked. Then the fire escape.

It gave them access to a window in the adjacent laboratory. The window was locked. Mark went back and returned presently with a long, thin-bladed knife. He found Marian waiting tensely on the fire escape. He turned the window lock with the knife.

They stepped gingerly into Moklokus' workrooms. Rooms crowded with intricately blown glass. Walking there in the near-blackness was dangerous.

They found another door beyond, opening into a short, pantrylike chamber filled with shelves of paraphernalia. And a second door at the end of that closet. Mark put his ear to it.

He heard voices, and recognized them.

Centora was talking softly, wickedly to Moklokus. "My dear Doctor, you were a close friend of Emerson Stickney's.

Your opinion will have immense weight. I want you simply to suggest that his holdings in Belgian Guiana be liquidated. I, myself, propose to take over the conduct of affairs there. And I am quite sure that you will do everything in your power to assist me."

Moklokus' response was faintly strained. "My dear Centora, *why* are you so certain that I'll help you plunder Stickney's estate?"

"I am very certain. You see, Dr. Moklokus, I happened to observe you in the act of filching Senator Prichard's trousers from his room while he was at dinner. From that I conclude that you murdered the worthy politician."

Moklokus spoke slowly. "And what other conclusions have you reached about me, Centora?"

"Merely that you were in a most uncomfortable predicament, which led you to do away with Stickney. And then, since your predicament was still somewhat uncomfortable, you thought that the suicide of a self-confessed murderer would be the most effective method of concealing"—he paused delicately—"whatever the little matter was you wished to conceal."

There was a pause. The Rumanian scientist replied almost lightly. "That's really very perceptive of you, Centora. You reason that I would feel the investigation certain to follow Stickney's murder might become embarrassing to me. That I would do away with Prichard, thereby removing suspicion from myself. However, since you knew that I had committed one murder—since you assumed I had committed two—I am rather surprised at your temerity in coming here to blackmail me tonight, Centora. In fact—"

Marian and Mark had not caught any noticeable change in Moklokus' tone. It was soft and polite. However, his speech was punctuated with a muffled explosion.

There was a moment of absolute silence.

Then the crumpling thud of a body.

After that a longer silence, broken by a new voice.

It was the voice of Emerson Stickney saying, "Drop that gun, Moklokus."

Mark, listening at the door, felt Marian shudder and sag as she heard her father speak. He put his arm around her.

On the other side of the door was an unimaginable scene. Moklokus had just shot Centora, and, suddenly, Stickney had appeared from the dead.

There was a long, soundless pause.

Then Moklokus broke it with words that trembled slightly. "Ah, Stickney! You've heard our conversation? I thought that when I shot Centora just now I had executed your murderer. But since you weren't murdered, I am rather at a loss—"

Stickney's voice was peaceful. "Centora thought you had killed me. You thought Centora had killed me. I'm surprised that you went to such pains to cover up a murder of which you were not guilty. It was adroit—but dangerous."

Moklokus answered, "Not so dangerous. If Centora had not spied me—" He sighed. "It is regrettable that I didn't get you, Emerson. The trunk. The refrigerator gas. But when I heard you were gone, I thought—"

"You thought Centora had done me in. Now, if you'll just come out from behind your desk—"

There was a sound of moving feet, and then the Rumanian spoke again, his voice suddenly vibrant. "Stickney, you will see that I am going to pick up my gun! Before you can get across the room to me! Isn't that light I see shining through the chambers of your revolver?"

"Don't move!" Stickney shouted. "One chamber is loaded."

Moklokus sighed. "Quite so. Your pistol is not loaded. Unfortunately for you, mine is, and now that I have picked it up and you have not shot me, I can complete the undertaking on which I have embarked. I have facilities here for disposing of any amount of biological waste. Your body as well as Centora's."

Stickney had tried to bluff him with an empty revolver and failed.

Moklokus was talking again. "Before I kill you, Emerson, I wish you would explain your appearance. Perhaps, when Centora hit you, you only feigned unconsciousness, and caught yourself on the rail of the deck below?"

"No," Stickney answered in an even tone. "If you're really interested in why I'm not dead—that is to say, why I am not yet dead—I'd be delighted to tell you."

"Please do."

Stickney began talking slowly, with remarkable calm. He talked to gain time in which to think. Talked to save his life, if it were possible.

"My maneuvers would appeal to you, Moklokus. I knew young Adams was making circuits of A deck. I went to the boat deck by the inside stairs. I wore gloves. I tied the rope. Then, between rounds of the young man, I took my post at the rail of A deck.

"When Adams appeared, I pretended to have been struck. I groaned. I toppled backwards, and then slid down the rope. One deck. I might have been seen. There might have been someone on the deck below. As a matter of fact, there was."

Mark and Marian, on the other side of the door, listened with frantic concentration. Moklokus was going to kill Marian's father—but he was in no hurry. And the financier was talking coolly, while part of his mind was unquestionably struggling for a way to escape being murdered.

Moklokus was aware of the fact. "Talk as much as you like, Stickney. Think as much as you like. I believe there is no way out of your present dilemma. But I am curious about one or two facts and I'd be grateful if you'd answer them before I kill you. You were saying that there was someone on the deck below?"

"It was Captain Ross."

"Ah!"

"The Captain has been my friend for a great many years. Earlier in the evening I explained to him that I was going to stage a fake murder."

"Why?"

"Because somebody was trying to kill me. You, for instance. I thought that if I were already dead it would frustrate my enemy. I assumed that by his actions after I had gone, I could identify him. Then I had another motive."

"Which was—?"

"Young Dr. Adams. I had become interested in him. I was anxious to see if he would be competent to handle my

182

affairs. It was imperative that I should know his full abilities and his basic character."

In the dark, behind the door, Mark knew what he would have to do. Stickney was coming to the end of the story. There was an even chance that the Rumanian's back would be to the door behind which Mark and Marian listened.

Mark would have to take that chance. He would have to open the door slowly and noiselessly—creep across the room—attack Moklokus.

Of course, Stickney—if it were Stickney who faced the door—would see the whole thing, and Stickney's eyes might betray the attempt. In that case, Moklokus would start shooting, and Mark and Marian's father would have only a slim chance. If it were Moklokus who faced the door, there would be no chance for either of them.

Mark seized the knob in tense fingers and began to turn it. Marian gripped his arm for an instant to indicate that she understood.

He opened the door a little.

Stickney's voice went on. "Yes, Dr. Moklokus, I wanted to test that young man. So I thought that while I was 'dead' I would let him be the dictator of my enterprises. And I am proud to say that Dr. Adams has done a magnificent job."

Mark had opened the door. He was able to look into the room. Moklokus, back toward him, was sitting at a desk twenty feet away.

Mark slid into the room. For a fraction of a second his eyes met Stickney's, and Mark's heart hammered with admiration: Stickney did not move a muscle of his face. He merely went on with his story as Mark inched toward Moklokus.

Stickney, in fact, arranged that story so that its most dramatic disclosure would surprise the Rumanian at the instant when Mark was ready to spring. "Of course, Captain Ross assisted me. It was in his own cabin that I hid. I heard your testimony to the Captain that established Dr. Adams' innocence. What was that, Moklokus? An effort to cast suspicion away from yourself? Or an attempt to ingratiate yourself with Dr. Adams when you found he had so much power?"

Moklokus answered lightly, "A little of both."

Mark had covered more than half the distance.

Stickney was nodding almost amiably. "You're a resourceful person. At the very outset of this business you almost got me. Twice. When I went, you thought Centora had done it. But as long as people would be probing my affairs in search of a murderer, your precious reputation was in jeopardy.

"So you provided a murderer—a dead one who couldn't defend himself. Not Centora. You were positive that he'd keep mum, and he was too slick to kill easily, anyway. Prichard . . . But I imagine you were quite surprised when I walked in here this evening."

"Surprised—and delighted."

"Naturally. It gives you the opportunity to settle everything, once and for all. But I will take the liberty of suggesting that from now on you beware of Dr. Adams. He is extremely competent. After my death—or even right now, for that matter—he will be dangerous."

Mark edged forward.

"You can doubtless give the proper psychological term to your particular brand of insanity," Stickney continued. "Megalomania—something like that. And this is your moment, isn't it? Too bad the gun Ross lent me is empty.

"And just one other thing, since I see you're getting impatient. I had an additional motive in pretending to have been murdered. Young Mark Adams was engaged to Miss Bates and—circumstances—had spoiled that engagement. I thought my 'death' would act as a powerful force to bring them back together. You see, Moklokus, my interest in Adams is not entirely detached. He is going to be my son-in-law."

"Son-in-law!" Moklokus was startled.

"Precisely. Miss Bates, my secretary, is actually my daughter."

"Daughter!"

"I'll explain that to you. I—"

Mark had covered the distance. He dove for the hand in which Moklokus held the gun. His chest crashed on the desk. He caught the wrist. The gun went off—but Stickney had dropped to the floor.

Moklokus was up and fighting. He had three times Mark's strength. But Mark hung on with desperation.

Then Stickney hit Moklokus behind the ear. He fell.

Marian was in her father's arms, crying.

Mark picked up the doctor's gun. He rubbed his shoulder and looked at the gun. When Moklokus tried to rise to his feet, Mark pointed it at him.

Nobody said anything. It wasn't necessary. Then Mark phoned for the police.

Marian was still weeping. But suddenly she went over to Mark and threw her arms around him. He kissed her. He patted her awkwardly, with the hand not holding the gun.

Stickney, keeping his eye on Moklokus, said in his easy voice, "You know, Mark, I've put you to something of a test. I didn't want a bust for a son-in-law. And about this wealth of mine. I had a friend who wanted desperately to fight in the last war. He could have had a commission. But he was one of the best publicity men alive. He knew that his propaganda work would be worth fifty men in the trenches. So he went into that work. You're geared for surgery and research, but also for a great deal more. If you can sacrifice a certain personal pride—which I think was like that other man's—"

Mark's eyes fell on the high-backed chair behind Moklokus' desk.

He knew that someday he would sit in that chair.

But the main thing was not that. The main thing was Marian, trembling in his arms.

"I still don't see how you knew enough to come here tonight. I—" Marian looked puzzled.

Mark grinned. "It was that stolen typewriter. I suddenly realized that the splash I heard had been made not by a body going overboard but by a typewriter! The splash would sound the same, and the typewriter would sink instantly. Of course, it was your father who 'stole' the typewriter.

"That meant your father was still alive—it made the whole rope trick plain as day. It meant Prichard had been murdered, as we suspected. He couldn't have 'confessed' to a crime that hadn't been committed.

"So I wanted to get immediately to Centora. When we heard he was here, I believed that he and Moklokus had worked together. I was sure neither of them knew your father was alive—otherwise, of course, Prichard wouldn't have been killed. So I wanted to hear what Centora and Moklokus had to say to each other."

"So did I," Stickney said. "I almost heard too much."

Outside, police sirens screeched in the distance. Moklokus shivered.

Mark took Marian's arm and led her toward the door. "It was all so obvious," he said.

She smiled—because it had not been obvious at all. But it *was* very satisfactory.

Ellery Queen has won five Edgars (the annual Mystery Writers of America awards similar to the Oscars of Hollywood), including the prestigious Grand Master award (1960); three MWA Scrolls and one Raven; and twice Queen was runner-up for the Best Novel of the Year award. He also has won both the gold and silver Gertrudes awarded by Pocket Books, Inc. Mystery writers of Japan gave Ellery Queen their gold-and-onyx Edgar Allan Poe ring, awarded to only five non-Japanese detective-story writers throughout the world. And in 1968 Iona College honored Queen with its Columba Prize in Mystery.

Ellery Queen is internationally known as an editor—*Ellery Queen's Mystery Magazine* is now in its 37th year of continuous publication.

The late Anthony Boucher, distinguished critic and novelist, described Queen best when he wrote: "Ellery Queen *is* the American detective story."

"Q"